Ginny Marlow's To Do...

1. Review depositions.

2. Prepare opening argument.

3. Pick up suits from dry cleaners.

4. Bust little sister out of small-town jail.

Ginny Marlow's List of Things NOT To Do...

1. Do not, under any circumstances, fall for the sexy sheriff who has arrested you for attempted bribery and sentenced you to ten days on his ranch!

2. Do not give in to his charming gestures and seductive smiles.

3. Do not let his happy family and good old-fashioned homespun advice get you thinking of leaving the big city for the simple pleasures of country livin'.

4. I repeat, DO NOT! (And good luck.)

Dear Reader,

The lure of the West is as strong today as it was a hundred years or more ago, when the wagon trains headed in that direction. I know I can't resist a cowboy. And when he's also a sheriff…! So is it any wonder that heroine Ginny Marlow finds herself inextricably entwined—and loving it!—with Quint Cutler? In *The Law and Ginny Marlow,* the latest in award-winner Marie Ferrarella's miniseries THE CUTLERS OF THE SHADY LADY RANCH, you'll see what happens when a quick trip out west turns into a lifetime of wide open spaces. You'll also be sorry there's only one more book to go in this wonderful family's story.

And if you've been following our cross-line miniseries FOLLOW THAT BABY—or even if you haven't— you've got a treat in store with Christie Ridgway's *The Millionaire and the Pregnant Pauper.* This homegrown Yours Truly star tells a romp of a tale—and takes you one book closer to the discovery of the missing Wentworth heir. Have a good time now, and next month travel to Silhouette Intimate Moments to see how the saga ends.

Have fun, and don't forget to come back next month for two more fun and fabulous books all about meeting— and marrying!—Mr. Right.

Yours,

Leslie J. Wainger
Executive Senior Editor

Please address questions and book requests to:
Silhouette Reader Service
U.S.: 3010 Walden Ave., P.O. Box 1325, Buffalo, NY 14269
Canadian: P.O. Box 609, Fort Erie, Ont. L2A 5X3

MARIE FERRARELLA

The Law and Ginny Marlow

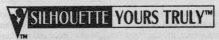

YOURS TRULY™

Published by Silhouette Books
America's Publisher of Contemporary Romance

To Emmy,
For all the joy you brought.

SILHOUETTE BOOKS

ISBN 0-373-52083-2

THE LAW AND GINNY MARLOW

Copyright © 1999 by Marie Rydzynski-Ferrarella

Printed in U.S.A.

Dear Reader,

I've always thought that there was something very sexy about a small-town sheriff putting himself on the line to protect his town. Sheriff Quint Cutler doesn't have to worry about any "bad guys" doing harm to the citizens of his town, Serendipity, Montana. But he does have to worry about a certain dark-haired, sharp lady lawyer laying claim to his heart—against her own will, as it turns out.

Geneva Marlow thought she was coming to Serendipity to rescue her sister; she had no idea that she was rescuing her heart from being doomed to a life of loneliness in the bargain. Orphaned long before her mother died, Ginny has always turned a brave face to the world and shouldered more than her share of responsibilities. Coming up against Quint Cutler and entering the warm world of the Cutler family reminded her of everything she was missing. Everything she wouldn't be missing if she only let love into her world.

Here's hoping you've found love in your world. Thank you for reading and being my audience.

Love,

Marie Ferrarella

Stop on by
The Shady Lady Ranch
in Serendipity, Montana,
home of the Cutler brood—five siblings finding love in the most unexpected places!

Zoe McKay m. Jake Cutler

Will Cutler m. Denise Cavanaugh
|
Audra Cavanaugh

Quint Cutler m. Geneva Marlow

Kent Cutler m. Brianne Gainsborough

Hank Cutler m. Fiona Reilly

Morgan Cutler m. ?

1

"**Y**ou have my little sister in your jail."

The declaration, coming from behind him, took Sheriff Quintin Cutler by surprise. Carly, his deputy, was out to lunch and Quint had thought himself alone in the small three-room jailhouse. Alone, save for the teenager cooling her heels and her attitude in the cell at the rear of the building.

The woman's voice sounded both angry and accusing. It also sounded like hot honey mixed with just the right amount of bourbon to go down smooth on a cold winter's night. It was the kind of voice that gave a man pause and made him try to visualize the sort of woman who would go with it.

She definitely wasn't from around here. He knew most of the people who lived in and around Serendipity, the small Montana town he'd been sheriff of these past four years. The second of five, Quint had always taken things at his own pace. He allowed himself a single moment to conjure up an image before he turned around to face reality and, most likely, disappointment. In a perfect world, the owner of the voice would be tall, he decided, on the slim side and sexier than he'd once thought those models in lingerie catalogs were.

Quint turned away from the bulletin board and the batch of new posters he was putting up. Pictures of runaways, every one of them. Sometimes it didn't seem quite real to him, all those kids taking off. Taking on a world that was, in all probability, a great deal tougher than anything they'd ever come across or imagined, just because there'd probably been some minor blowup at home.

The girl he had in the cell in back was a runaway. Not as hopeless, not as dirty as some he'd encountered, but a definite runaway. He knew the signs. Her sister's timing impressed him. Though she'd been in town a couple of days, the girl had only been in his cell for a matter of a few hours.

Finally looking at the owner of the voice, he smiled to himself.

Damn, but he was good, Quint thought. Looked like some things were meant to be perfect after all. The woman who stood in his office, her fisted hands on her designer-covered, shapely hips, was as close to the vision he'd imaged as anything could be. Maybe a little bit better. She had medium-length dark brown hair that curled and swirled about her face like warm waves of water and eyes the color of emeralds at first light.

Right now, those emeralds were shooting sparks

at him. He figured if they'd been bullets, he would have been dead by now.

But he would have gone with a smile. She was, as his father liked to say, one hell of a looker.

Quint raised an eyebrow, noting the air of barely harnessed impatience mingled with frustration about the woman. Fresh from some big city, he judged, and hell-bent to get back.

"You mean the little girl who was caught stealing from Joe Taylor's general store this morning?" In sharp contrast to hers, his own voice was calm as he put the question to her.

Geneva Marlow raised her chin. It almost looked as if she was on the attack, Quint thought.

Ginny was, though she tried to hide it, also on just this side of frantic, having worried herself sick about Jenny. That didn't put her in the most reasonable frame of mind as she faced the sheriff.

She didn't like this man's attitude. That laid-back pose wasn't fooling her. Experienced, she smelled a shakedown coming on. She was surprised he hadn't asked the question with his hand out.

"I mean my sister, Jennifer Marlow, who has been sitting in your jail, according to a reliable witness, since eight this morning."

The evenness of her own voice surprised her, given the state her nerves were in. Ginny had been haunted by the thought that she'd never see Jenny again, all because of a stupid argument over an even stupider boy who, Ginny had maintained, was a horrible influence on her sister. She'd been right, but right was a poor consolation to coming home and finding that her sister had taken off for parts unknown rather than be separated from Kyle.

Quint's smile, like his words, was deliberately slow in making its appearance. He could see that it irritated her. She made him think of a prize stallion, pawing the ground, raring to run him over.

"Reliable witness," Quint echoed innocently. He knew exactly who she was referring to. "You must mean Jeremiah Stone."

That Jeremiah was a character, Quint thought. Jeremiah Stone was Serendipity's resident philosopher and all-round busybody. He spent his days sitting just outside of Taylor's General Store, whittling, rocking and talking to anyone who chanced to walk by. Man, woman, child or beast, it made no matter to him. If they had ears, he'd talk to them. Jeremiah was practically a fixture, watching the comings and goings of everyone in Serendipity. He'd been retired as long as Quint or anyone in town could remember, although no one was really sure from what since no one could recall ever seeing Jeremiah put in a day's work anywhere.

"Yes." Ginny had gotten the man's name and more information than she'd needed when she stopped to talk to him. Agitated though she was, she'd recorded all the pertinent particulars on the back pages of her planner.

She wanted to make sure there were no delays in

getting Jenny out. She hadn't counted on a sheriff who spoke as if each word was costing him a portion of his paycheck. "I spoke with Mr. Stone before coming here."

Quint nodded. The woman must have had someone else track her sister. She was far too neat and pressed to have been on the road herself, conducting the search. "Well, he steered you right. We've got a Jenny Marlow in the back, in one of the cells."

As Ginny opened her mouth to ask for the terms of Jenny's release, the sheriff took out several packages of cupcakes from his middle desk drawer and tossed them on his desk. Ginny looked at him questioningly.

"She tried to walk out without paying for these." Quint shook his head. He had no doubts that this was what Jenny was subsisting on. "Nothing but sugar here. With a diet like that, no wonder the girl's bouncing off the walls in there."

Ginny felt the last of her valued patience shredding. Jenny was hers to find fault with, not this two-bit sheriff who sounded as if he hadn't managed to wander into the latter half of the century yet. Ginny's eyes narrowed. "Most likely what has her bouncing off the walls is the injustice of being held in jail for something so minor."

The sheriff raised his eyes to hers. Ginny found she couldn't readily draw them away. "How much should she have stolen before you'd think it was major?''

Had she been in a more reasonable frame of mind, she would have allowed that she deserved that. Stealing was stealing and she'd never condoned it. But the past few weeks had left her almost sleepless and exceptionally high-strung. She wasn't thinking as clearly as she might have been, but she wasn't about to admit it to the likes of him.

Temper had her setting her mouth hard. ''That's not the point, Sheriff.''

He nodded. ''You're right. The point is—can't do the time, don't do the crime.''

Ginny rolled her eyes. If she'd had time to get breakfast this morning before dashing to make the plane that brought her here from L.A. after she'd gotten Carmichael's phone call saying the detective had located Jenny, it would be in danger of coming up.

''Oh, please, spare me. We're looking at three dollars' worth of goods.''

''Two-fifty,'' Quint corrected her amiably. He ignored the dark look she gave him. ''They were on sale.''

''Whatever.'' Exasperated with him, angry at Jenny for putting her through hell and angrier at herself for somehow failing Jenny and making her take this drastic step to begin with, Ginny took her wallet out of her shoulder bag. She jerked out the first bill she came to, glanced to see what it was, then held it out to him. It was a five. "I'll pay full price—with interest. Now if you'll just let her go—"

The woman was accustomed to getting her way, Quint judged. He was beginning to see the origins of the problem between her and her sister. Quint made no attempt to reach for the money.

Instead, he sat on the edge of his desk, his hands folded in front of him as if he had all the time in the world. "'Fraid I can't do that."

"Why not?"

Her eyes narrowed. Ginny knew exactly why not. These small-town officers of the law were all alike. Officers of the law, that was laughable. More like abusers of the law. This sheriff was no different than the one in the town where she and Jenny had lived the first part of their lives. Smoke Tree, Arizona, a town that could easily fit into anyone's back pocket. He had been just out for what he could get, legally or otherwise. Dealings with Sheriff Dewey had left a very bad taste in her mouth. One that would last her a lifetime.

Dewey owned half the town outright and blackmailed the other half into submission. Knowing him was one of the things that had sent her into law in the first place. People like that had to be put in their place. It was only when corporate law beckoned, promising to help her pay off her mountain of a school loan more quickly, that she'd put her principles on hold. For a while.

"Do you want more money?"

"How much money would you be willing to give?" In spite of his question, the planes of his broad, chiseled face appeared completely innocent. She knew it.

It was a scam, just as she'd thought. And this man in front of her, all six-two or -three of him, with the dark blond hair that brushed against the top of his collar and the shiny tin star, was nothing more than a con artist. Just like Dewey. If she had the time, she'd have him up on charges so fast, his gorgeous head would be spinning.

But she didn't have the time. She really didn't even have the time to come here and pick Jenny up. But it wasn't something she felt she could trust anyone else to do. Handling Jenny was not an easy matter. Even she was failing miserably at it and she loved Jenny more than anything in the world.

"All right, I have—" Ginny didn't bother pausing to count the money in her wallet, she knew exactly what she'd brought with her. Cash, rather than plastic because cash was what people trusted in small towns like this. "Five hundred dollars in here." Extracting the bills, she slapped them down on his desk. "Is that enough to buy my sister's freedom?"

Quint let out a low whistle. There were ten fifty-dollar bills practically fanned out on his stained blotter. "That's a lot of money to be carrying around." Apparently this woman believed she could solve everything with money. He wondered if she ever sat down and talked to her sister, or if she'd just thrown money at any problem that had arisen in hopes that it would just fade away beneath the weight of the bills. "Someone might rob you if they knew you were running around with that much money."

Someone already has, Ginny thought. "I know." Her eyes deliberately fixed on his for a moment. "Now will you open the cell and let her out?"

Quint picked up the bills, arranged them in a neat pile, then handed them back to the woman. "No."

Ginny stared at the bills. "What?" What was his game? Did he think he could shake her down for more?

"No." Quint enunciated the single word slowly, then smiled at her. "Better?"

Anger, barely contained before, all but exploded now inside Ginny. She'd spent the past two and a half weeks alternating between being worried half out of her mind about Jenny and being furious with her for having done something so stupid. Ginny was in no mood for whatever this man had up his sleeve.

"No, it's not better," she informed him tersely. "And what do you mean, no?" She held the money out to him, giving him one last chance.

He acted as if she'd already put the bills away. "No means no. It's really not that hard a word to figure out," he said conversationally. "Not like antidisestablishmentarianism." The grin, had she been more receptive, would have been engaging. But as it was, it was merely incredibly provoking to her. As was he. "Now there's a word that never made any sense to me. Just something I figure they thought up to—"

He was going to go on talking forever, wasn't he? The last thin thread of patience she had left snapped. "Forgive me, Sheriff, but I really don't care to hear about your philosophy on words. I'm hot, I'm tired, I've driven across half this state trying to get to my sister and all I want to do is take her and get out of here." The look in her eyes dared him to say no again. "Now, are you going to let her out or not?"

Acting as if he were selecting an appetizer from a tray being offered him, Quint chose the word he wanted out of her question. "'Not.'"

Ginny could have screamed and very nearly did. She struggled to hold on to her temper. Maybe if she pretended she was in court, facing a worthy adversary, instead of in a small-town jailhouse, staring up at a man who was the very definition of maddening, she might stand a better chance at controlling her temper.

"Why?"

Quint crossed his arms before him. "Your sister, ma'am, has a bad attitude."

That was the second time he'd addressed her with that pseudopoliteness. She wasn't buying it. "My name isn't ma'am."

He nodded. "I don't rightly know what your name is, seeing as how you never introduced yourself before making accusations."

Ginny gritted her teeth together. "It wasn't an accusation, it was a fact. My sister is in your jail. Now, are you or aren't you going to let her out?"

Quint was beginning to suspect she could shoot lightning bolts out of those eyes of hers if she wanted. The angrier she grew, the calmer he became. Someone had to maintain the balance here, he thought. "Strictly speaking, it isn't my jail, it's—"

"I don't care!"

Ginny pressed her lips together. Shouting wasn't going to get her anywhere. She knew that, would have been the first to point that out, under different circumstances. But it was just that her nerves were in tatters. She was under an extreme amount of pressure to return to L.A. Lately it felt as if her self-control was being peeled away from her inch by inch, like the skin of a banana. The firm, representing Twain Dynamics, had one of its biggest cases coming to court and Leary, the senior partner, was counting on her to make a good showing. She didn't have time to waste exchanging words with this infuriating man.

Ginny took a second to collect herself. She had no idea why Jenny wanted to hurt her this way, but whatever her sister's reasons were, she didn't want Jenny running around out on her own. At seven-

teen, Jenny was still a minor, and as far from being
an adult emotionally as a cow was from dancing
the lead in *Swan Lake.* The trouble Jenny had gotten herself into in this two-by-four town clearly underscored her point.

Ginny took a deep breath then let it out slowly,
and tried to look as contrite as she could allow herself to be under the circumstances.

"I'm sorry, I didn't mean to shout at you, it's
just that I really am very tired. I've been trying to
find Jenny for almost three weeks." Ginny bit her
lower lip for effect. He probably liked playing the
big, strong hero. It only cost her a little to let him
think he was. "She ran away from home."

Quint nodded, still playing the stumbling bump-
kin the lady took him for. "I kind of figured that
out on my own."

Maybe he could be made to come around after
all, Ginny thought, relieved. It was about time
something finally went her way.

The phrase echoed in her head.

It seemed ironic to feel that way. From the outside, Ginny knew she appeared to have everything
going her way. She was an up-and-coming corporate attorney in line for a possible junior partnership
at a well-respected L.A.-based law firm. She had
risen above daunting circumstances, gotten an education and not only provided for herself and for
her sister, but also provided well. She was a far cry

from the devastated, newly orphaned Arizona teenager she'd once been.

And yet, happiness and peace of mind continued to elude her.

Continued to elude her because the better circumstances became, the more her relationship deteriorated with the sister she had been both mother and father to. It was as if Jenny resented her success. Nine years her junior, her sister seemed to relish going out of her way to make her life a living hell. Over the past couple of years, communication between them vacillated between bad and nonexistent. And Jenny had changed. Drastically. First there'd been the dropping grades, then the friends Ginny had warned Jenny against, the friends Jenny stubbornly refused to give up. Like Kyle.

Running away had been the last straw.

Ginny had put her entire life on hold, not to mention quite possibly jeopardizing her career, to come and bring her home after the detective she'd hired had tracked Jenny down.

Now, to top it all off, this muscle-bound man with a badge was giving her grief.

Desperate, Ginny went against her principles and tried flattery.

"Well, you figured right, but then you're probably accustomed to that." She drew closer to him, searching for his good side and praying he had one. "I really am running horribly behind, so if you could just let her go…"

She smelled good, Quint thought. Something pricey and tempting, guaranteed to make a man take notice. As if she needed that. Everything about the woman made a man sit up and take notice.

Quint held his ground as she placed a supplicating hand on his arm. There were things at stake here that couldn't be swept away and ignored.

"I already told you," he said, the amiable smile on his lips never fading, "I can't do that."

Annoyed, embarrassed by his smile, Ginny stared at him. "You can't be serious. You're really going to hold my sister in jail for stealing four packages of cupcakes?"

He nodded. He had no doubt that Joe Taylor could be convinced to drop the charges. But the girl inside the cell needed something more important than her freedom right now. "For that, and for her attitude."

Her attitude? Where did he get off, damning her sister and putting her into a jail cell because he didn't like her attitude? Ginny made no attempt to hide the indignation she felt.

"And since when is a bad attitude a reason for imprisonment?"

Maybe bad attitudes ran in the family, Quint thought. This woman could certainly stand a little attitude adjustment herself. "Since maybe she could put the time in jail to good use and cool off a bit."

Ginny couldn't believe it. He *was* serious. "That's not what jails are for."

Where she came from, Quint was sure only hardened criminals saw the inside of a cell. It was different out here. "Know a lot about jails, do you?"

Ginny really didn't care for his tone. If he asked her, *he* was the one who could stand to have his attitude reworked. He was mocking her.

"I'm an attorney."

That explained a great deal. Quint had never had much use for lawyers. They tended to be enamored with their own importance. "Ah."

Finally. She'd gotten through. He was probably afraid she'd sue his butt off. The idea was not without its merits. But she had a sister to bail out and a plane to catch.

"Yes, 'ah.' Listen, Sheriff, surely we can come to some sort of understanding before either one of us gets too old to stand up." She couldn't help the sarcasm that wrapped itself around her words. He'd pushed her past the limit of good manners with his concerned-sheriff act.

Quint almost laughed, but knew that wouldn't be appreciated. "You certainly are testy."

All right, since they were making observations and being honest, she could fire one in kind back at him. "And you certainly are annoying."

If she was trying to get him angry, Quint was afraid he was going to disappoint her. Growing up with his brothers and sister had taught him all about the merits of hanging on to his temper. He figured if he could put up with Morgan, he could put up with any woman. Even one who acted so cock-sure of herself as this one.

"Just playing by the rules, ma'am."

"Drop the hayseed act, my name is Geneva Marlow."

"Pretty name, Geneva." Unusual, he mused. It fit her.

"Thank you." Ginny bit off the words. She glanced at her watch. Time was growing short. "Now I'd like to pay my sister's fine and get out of here."

Once again, he shook his head. "Can't do that."

Ginny felt as if she was stuck in someone's idea of a joke. Or a science-fiction story where the characters were destined to go around and around the same point until the end of time.

"And why not?" She stopped herself from shouting the words at the last minute.

The lady's buttons were definitely close to the surface, Quint realized. He wondered how often she and the girl in the back got into shouting matches. Probably too often. Still, she'd come looking for her, expressing concern. That meant there had to be some sort of an emotional bond between them. Perhaps even love. Too bad neither one seemed consciously aware of that.

"Simple," he explained. "Fine hasn't been set yet."

Was he deliberately acting like a half-wit, or had she overestimated his brain capacity? Ginny wondered. It wouldn't be the first time a hunk of a man turned out to have next-to-nothing between his ears.

"So set it," she told him. The innocent look on his face, in her estimation, was wearing a bit thin.

"You being an attorney and all, you'd know that I can't do that. It's up to the judge."

Yes, she knew that. Knew, too, that he was doing this on purpose. "Then get him, please."

Quint noticed that her lips barely moved. He made no effort to go. "Can't. He's on vacation."

Now Ginny was convinced. "Are you deliberately trying to annoy me?"

"Not deliberately." And then he smiled. It was a rich smile, the kind that took in everything within range. Ginny tried not to react to it. It was all undoubtedly part of his scam. "Well, maybe, but you can see how annoying it is to talk to someone who's got the wrong answer to everything, now can't you?"

She'd had just about all of him she could take. Mentally, she began framing the letter registering her complaint about this misrepresenter of the law to the nearest person in authority.

"Your point?"

Quint spelled it out for her. "Your sister acted pretty much that way when I tried to talk to her, except she didn't smile like I just did."

Ginny's mouth dropped open. That did it. The sooner she got Jenny and herself out, the better.

"We'll take points off her score for that," she promised. "Now what do I have to do to get her out of jail?"

That answer, in Quint's estimation, was even simpler. "Wait."

This had to be the most infuriating man on the face of the earth. "Wait? For what? Hell to freeze over?" She took his hand and turned it, palm up. "I know a scam when I see one, Sheriff, and this is a scam, but I don't have time to fight the forces of evil. I have a real case to prepare for and a trial date breathing down my neck, so just take this money and let my sister out. Then you can go back to doing whatever it was you were doing before I walked in. Putting up posters, or scratching yourself, I don't care—"

The look in his eyes brought her tirade to an abrupt halt.

"If you mean scratching my head, I do that on occasion, particularly when I'm puzzled. Like now, because I'm trying to figure out why a lady like you would act in a manner that wasn't befitting to her."

She hadn't a clue what he was talking about. "I'm sure all this is very fascinating but I don't have time to hear this."

"Oh, but you do." Taking hold of her arm, Quint gently but firmly escorted her to the rear of the building. "You're going to have a lot of time to hear things. Especially your sister when she talks. I figure that might be the problem in a nutshell. Neither one of you is taking the time to listen."

She struggled, trying to shrug him off. She could have saved her effort. "Just what are you implying?" Ginny demanded.

Jenny was on her feet the moment she saw Ginny. Tears of relief formed and dried in an instant, replaced by the bravado that had become the younger girl's armor. "About time you got here. Get me out of this cage, Ginny."

"Ginny?" Quint looked from Jenny to Ginny, waiting for an explanation.

"It's my nickname," she said tersely. "Now, can we get on with this?" Again, Ginny tried to pull her arm away, but found that his grip, though gentle, was completely unshakable.

"Absolutely. Step back, please." Waving at Jenny, he waited until she complied. When she did, he unlocked the cell. But instead of allowing Jenny to come out, with one deft movement, he pushed Ginny in.

The door clanged into place. He locked it again.

It all happened so fast that, for a moment, Ginny could only stare at him in complete shock. "What do you think you're doing?"

Quint smiled patiently. "I'd think that would be plain, Miss Marlow. I'm arresting you."

It took everything she had not to sputter. "On what charge?"

His smile widened. Ginny had a very uneasy feeling, watching it spread on his lips. Something told her she was in real trouble.

"We'll skip the part about mouthing off and go straight to attempted bribery of an officer of the law," Quint answered. "Get comfortable, ladies. Looks like you've got a long day ahead of you. I suggest you spend it ironing out your differences."

"You can't be serious."

"Oh, but I can."

Turning, he walked away, grinning to himself.

2

The sound of a raised female voice met his ears even before Carly Cutler had a chance to pull the outer jailhouse door completely open. The girl his cousin Quint had brought in earlier this morning sounded madder than his mother had the time she'd caught him and Suzee Daltry in the hayloft.

Closing the door behind him, Carly winced as the voice rose another decibel. He could have sworn it changed pitch, as well. Maybe they had a real mental case on their hands, although on first glance, she didn't look it. Just mad, real mad.

He caught his cousin's eye and looked at Quint, his handsome, uncomplicated features settling into a puzzled frown.

"Is that girl yelling at herself, Quint?" He dropped his hat on the desk. "Sounds like we've got ourselves more than we bargained for with that one."

Quint thought of the other woman in the cell. The one who looked like a long, tall glass of cool water on a hot day. Made a man realize how thirsty he could get without even knowing it.

"You might say that." Quint leaned back at his desk. "She's not yelling at herself, by the way. She's yelling at her sister."

"Sister?" The frown dissolved into a look of utter mystification. "You mean there's two of them back there now?" When he'd left, Carly mused, there had only been the girl, Jenny. The three cells in back were usually kept empty. One of them was used as a storage area and he occasionally availed himself of one of the remaining ones as a temporary bedroom whenever he spent the night in town. Occupants were a rarity, two was unheard of. "When did that happen?"

Quint smiled at his cousin's phrasing. Just a week older than Morgan, Carly possessed all the innocence that Quint's sister didn't. Whenever he looked at Carly, Quint was reminded of all that was good and uncomplicated in the world. Quint had a suspicion that Carly was living out some childhood fantasy, being deputy to his sheriff. Too many Western novels as a kid, he supposed, but there was no harm in it.

Quint glanced at the overhead clock. It was well into the afternoon. Carly had made his lunch break into a prolonged event—again.

"Almost an hour ago."

Carly grinned sheepishly. The voices in the back

were getting more intense. Curiosity was getting the better of him.

"Can you show me how you did that?" He nodded toward the door leading to the rear of the building, taking a step toward it. "Making one girl into two? Might make for a neat trick. Might even get myself a date for your brother's wedding that way." His blue eyes shone. "Can't find a girl, just conjure one up."

As if Carly had ever had trouble finding female companionship, Quint thought, amused. Women had always been drawn to Carly, wanting to mother him. That attitude quickly changed once they were in his company. Mothering became the furthest thing from their minds.

In that, Carly was every inch a Cutler, except that no one had ever wanted to mother him, Quint thought. Neither he nor any of his brothers even remotely resembled the type that stirred a woman's mothering instincts. Judging by the way his brothers were dropping like flies, a great many other instincts were being stirred lately—on everyone's part. It was, he thought, going to be a very interesting winter. A lot of available ladies were going to be out there now that his brothers had dropped out of the game.

"Sorry to burst your hopes, Carly." Quint rose from his chair. "But there was no conjuring involved." Although, he had to admit, if he did have any conjuring abilities, Ginny Marlow would be just the kind of woman he'd want to conjure up for himself. The kind of woman who could heat up a cold Montana night just with the look in her eyes alone. "Geneva Marlow came looking for her sister."

She didn't look like a Geneva, Quint decided. Ginny suited her much better. Geneva sounded too aloof and, judging from that hot tongue of hers, if you scratched that aloofness, you were going to get a hell of a lot of emotion for your trouble.

Might be worth it, too, he mused, his mouth curving ever so slightly at the thought.

The argument in the back, whatever it was about, was escalating. Carly strained to make out the words, but all he could hear was the pitch and the timbre. Concern penciled in light lines along his mouth.

His eyes shifted toward Quint. "Shouldn't you be there in case things get ugly?"

Ugly, now there was a word that neither one of those two women would ever hear in their lifetime, Quint thought. Not unless something really drastic happened to change things.

He placed a hand over the keys that Carly was reaching for. "I don't think those two will come to blows. The older one has invested too much time and effort in tracking the younger one down. You don't do that unless you really love somebody."

A shriek of frustration rattled the windows. Carly

looked skeptical. "Doesn't exactly sound like love to me."

"Love has many sounds, Carly." Quint picked up the ring of keys and toyed with them. "Besides, I thought I'd give them both a chance to work things out for a while."

"Is that why you're out here instead of in there?"

It was evident that Carly was dying for a look. Quint nodded in reply to his question. "Neither one seemed very keen on my hanging around and refereeing." He grinned broadly. "Made me feel a little safer to have the bars between us."

"What did you arrest the other one for?"

"She tried to bribe me to let Jenny go."

He hadn't taken it seriously, of course, although he knew she meant it seriously at the time. If he'd allowed himself to get insulted every time someone threw a sarcastic barb in his direction, or an outsider took a superior attitude, he'd never have time for anything else. He'd just used it as an excuse to put the two women together.

"Bribe you?" This sounded like big-city corruption to Carly. To his knowledge, nobody bribed anyone in Serendipity. "How much?"

There was almost a note of wistfulness in Carly's voice. Quint tried not to laugh. "Doesn't matter. What matters is that there are two women on the other side of that door who need to find out how to resolve some of the problems facing them."

Carly had done part of his growing up on the Cutler's Shady Lady Ranch. It had been a den of constant yelling, competition and more than occasional brawling. This included Morgan, who for a while fancied herself more of a man than any of her brothers, except for Quint. She'd outgrown it, or at least partially so, by the time she'd entered her second decade. But for his own pride's sake, Carly knew enough to stay clear of Morgan when her temper was running hot.

Like the tempers in the back. "Doesn't sound like there's very much resolving going on."

Quint sighed. You would have thought that after almost an hour, they would have run out of steam and started making sense.

"Nope," he agreed, "there doesn't. Looks like they might be here for the day." That being the case, there were a few arrangements he was going to have to see to making.

Quint wondered if his mother was still as understanding as she used to be.

Ginny closed her eyes, trying to gather strength. Exhaustion had come and gone, and she was riding the crest of her second wind. It was becoming a way of life, plumbing the depths for just a little more energy, a little more endurance. A little more patience.

This time she was coming up empty.

The angry look on Jenny's face picked apart the

unraveling ends of what was left of her temper. Ginny had to struggle not to let the full force of it loose.

Why was it that with the person who mattered most in her life she could never put into words what she was feeling? Couldn't make Jenny somehow understand if not everything, then enough to resolve this uneasy schism between them and bring about its end? Ginny was dynamite when it came to putting together briefs or standing up in court and addressing the jury or the judge. But none of those skills seemed to stick when it came to talking to Jenny.

There didn't seem to be a right way to talk to the girl anymore, she thought, fighting frustration. Or a right way to approach her for that matter.

Despair, dressed in anger, coaxed a fresh round of words from her mouth. "How could you do such a stupid thing? Running away never solved anything. Do you have any idea what could have happened to you? Any idea at all?"

When she thought of all the things that could have happened to her sister out on the road all alone, she wanted to cry. Most of all, she wanted to shake Jenny until her brains fell into place again.

Jenny raised her chin, daggers shooting from her eyes. There was only the slightest hint of hurt. "To you everything I do is stupid."

She was probably just imagining the hurt, Ginny thought. Lately Jenny was far too tough-skinned to be hurt by anything she said. She was the one whose heart was bleeding.

"No, not everything, but this certainly was." Ginny curled her hands into fists, keeping them on her hips since pummeling Jenny into the ground was tempting but unthinkable. "You can't deny that."

The look on the young face was almost savage. "I can deny any damn thing I want. You think because you pay for my things, you own me."

It seemed they were doomed to go around this point again. Where had Jenny gotten such a ridiculous idea? She'd never remotely said anything to make her sister feel that way.

"I never wanted to own you, but you do owe me—"

Jenny's head jerked up, triumph in her eyes as she won her point. "Ha!"

Why was every exchange of words a battle? Why couldn't they just talk? Ginny looked at her sister's face and searched for the girl she used to know. "You owe me some respect."

Bitterness twisted Jenny's young mouth.

"It's a two-way street," Jenny spat out.

Ginny wanted to lash out at her. Instead, she managed to keep her cool. "When you do something I can respect, I will."

"Right." Arms crossed, Jenny swung away from her sister, only to see the sheriff standing there. She hadn't heard him come in. "Well, what are you looking at?"

Annoyance rose another notch inside Ginny. She'd taught her sister better than this. "Jenny, you can't mouth off at an officer of the law, that's what got you here in the first place."

Jenny shot Ginny a hostile glare over her shoulder, tossing her head. Long, brown hair swept along her shoulders. "You should talk."

"Yes, I should." She'd be damned if her sister was going to continue embarrassing her this way. "I've got more experience than you do."

Anger succeeded in nudging away the last of Jenny's fear. Once her sister had turned up, the specter that had ridden along with her like a silent, ghoulish companion slowly began to slip away. Jenny's eyes grew into smug slits as she regarded Ginny.

"Seems to me we're both in the same boat. On the inside of this two-bit cell, looking out at a two-bit sheriff." She flounced down on the bunk. "Fat lot of good your experience did either one of us, much less you."

Quint appeared completely unaffected by the exchange, other than to seem mildly amused. "I see we're not making any progress here."

Ginny's look was frosty as her eyes swept in his direction. She didn't care for the pronoun he was carelessly bandying about at her expense.

"I don't know about you, but I'm not," she replied icily. "She's been like this for the last year. Two," she amended.

Jenny resented being referred to in the third person. "I didn't think you noticed anything about me."

Pouting, Jenny slanted a long look toward the man standing behind the sheriff. She wondered if the deputy was his younger brother. They looked kind of alike, not like her and Ginny. She looked nothing like Ginny, she thought. Ginny was the pretty one, the one who always got all the attention. The one who would have looked good climbing out of a mud puddle.

Ginny stared at her. How could Jenny say something so stupid? Did she actually believe that? "I noticed everything about you."

Jenny rolled her eyes and made a noise between her teeth that indicated her feelings on the subject. "How could you, you're always working, always at the office from dawn to midnight. You even sleep there."

Yeah, Quint thought, he would have pegged her as a workaholic. The conservative suit, the no-nonsense attitude. The "in a hurry" attitude. But the hair, he thought, the hair that tumbled about her face like a dark chocolate storm indicated that there was still definitely hope of getting her to cross over.

He nodded toward the pouting teenager, his eyes on Ginny. "Sounds like she might have a reason for her grievances."

Ginny flung him a warning look. It was bad enough he had them locked up for his own amusement. This was a family matter and something he had no business interfering with. "I'll thank you to keep out of this."

The lady looked positively lethal, Quint thought. Made him kind of glad he'd never have to be on the wrong side of the table opposite her in court. He bet she was dynamite, strutting her stuff.

"Sorry, I'm here to uphold the peace, and from what I've been hearing, there isn't much peace to uphold inside here. Maybe the two of you might feel better on a full stomach."

He'd probably slip something into the food. She wouldn't put it past him. Ginny remembered what Sheriff Dewey had been like back in Smoke Tree.

"I'll feel better once we're out of here," Ginny said tersely.

But Quint shook his head. "Not from what I just overheard."

She couldn't believe this was happening. "There's a little thing called the Bill of Rights that says you can't keep us here indefinitely." Ginny could feel Jenny's eyes on her, waiting to see what she did next.

"That's true," he allowed, but he made no move to open the cell.

Ginny felt like screaming. She wrapped her hands around the bars, coming as close to the infuriating man as the barrier allowed. Bill of Rights notwithstanding, she and Jenny were at this man's mercy unless she could get help.

"I have a phone call coming."

Quint nodded slowly, as if he were mulling it over. "That you do." He could see the fury building in her eyes. She had beautiful eyes, he thought. Even if they were shooting sparks. Or maybe because of it.

Unlocking the door, he stepped back to let Ginny out. But when Jenny bolted to her feet and made a beeline for the exit a second later, he placed his hand up, blocking her way.

"Not you, little one. We've only got the one phone."

"Figures." Jenny spat out the word. She did it strictly on principle. There was no one she knew to call who could get her out of this jam, or even come—other than the woman who was already sharing the cell with her. If there had been someone to call, she wouldn't have hitched her way up here to this godforsaken place after that jerk Kyle ran off with the last of her money, leaving her stranded.

She glared at Quint as he closed the cell door again and locked it.

"Keep an eye on her, Carly. She looks like a slick one." With a knowing smile, Quint winked in Jenny's direction as he carefully escorted her sister out.

Shooting a frustrated, disgusted look at Carly, Jenny flounced back on the bunk. Carly leaned against the back wall, content to do exactly what Quint told him to and just look at Jenny until the others returned. He'd had worse assignments.

Shutting the door that separated the cells from the office behind him, Quint indicated the black object on his desk. An antique in today's world, the telephone, he found, was not without its charm.

"There's the phone."

Ginny stared down at it. She'd only seen its likeness in an old photograph she had of her late grandmother. "A rotary dial?" She circled the desk, as if not certain how to approach the telephone. "Who does this office belong to, Alexander Graham Bell?"

If she meant to rile him, she was going to have to do a lot better than that, he thought. "Came with the office. I figured it had a lot of history attached to it." He knew for a fact that it had sat there since Serendipity had *had* a sheriff's office. "I'm big on history."

Ginny bit her tongue from uttering the first retort that came to mind. Not that it made any sense, it would just let her vent some of the frustration she was feeling. But that would do absolutely no good.

What she'd said to her sister was true. It wouldn't do to antagonize the sheriff although the thought was sorely tempting.

Very gingerly, expecting the phone to fall apart at any second, she placed her fingers in the holes one at a time and dialed. Ginny watched in veiled fascination as the dial returned to its original position each time with a smart little "click." On its last go-round, she actually heard the phone on the other end ringing.

Raising her eyes, she saw that the sheriff was watching her. It took effort not to shift. "I'm surprised this thing works."

His smile was easy and engaging as she leaned a hip against the edge of the desk. "Lot of things around here might surprise you."

She raised a brow as she waited for the pickup on the other end. If this man thought to impress her, he was mistaken.

"I doubt that, and I'd appreciate a little privacy." She gestured him away.

Amiable, Quint moved aside, but he took care not to let her out of his sight. He figured she wasn't going anywhere without her sister, but that was about all he felt confident about.

Ginny's heart sank. When the other end finally picked up, she heard a recorded message telling her that there was no one available to take her call right now.

She grabbed the receiver with both hands, willing someone to miraculously materialize.

"Cliff, are you there? Cliff, if you are, pick up. Pick up the phone, Cliff! This is Geneva Marlow. I'm stuck in—" Suddenly blank, she looked at the man who was her jailer.

"Serendipity," Quint supplied easily.

Ginny rolled her eyes. The town's moniker was a complete and utter misnomer.

"Serendipity, Montana. The number here is—" She looked at the faded, perfectly structured numbers on the dial and recited them into the receiver. She was surprised that they were so clear and so neat. "Damn," she swore as she heard the machine cut her off before she was able to give the last number.

All right, so her assistant wasn't there. She'd just call David Fontaine. It would give the junior partner a laugh, but right now, she was desperate. She'd deal with the consequences of this later.

She'd only managed to dial one number before the sheriff placed his hand in the way. It wasn't a very large hand, not the kind belonging to a Neanderthal, but it looked exceptionally capable of keeping her from dialing.

"What are you doing?" he asked mildly.

Maybe he was just simpleminded. "Making another call."

Quint shook his head. Very deliberately, he removed the telephone from beneath her hand and placed it on another part of the desk. "'Fraid not. The law allows for one call."

She had to struggle not to sputter. He made her so angry, she was having trouble seeing straight. "But it was an answering machine."

Very carefully, he took hold of her elbow, guiding her back to the rear of the jail and the cells.

"The law doesn't say there has to be someone breathing on the other end when it's picked up, it just says one call."

If that wasn't the most pigheaded, infuriating... She stopped to collect herself and took a deep breath. There was nothing to be gained by telling him what she thought of him and his strong-arm ways. That could keep until she and Jenny were out of here.

"All right, I don't need David." Ginny's voice was terse, strained. "I can represent myself *and* my sister." If he grinned any harder, that granite head of his was going to crack, sending all the rocks he had within it tumbling out. "Okay," she demanded wearily, "what are you smiling about?"

"Nothing, I just recalled that old line about the man who represents himself in court has a fool for a client." She looked like a volcano about to erupt, Quint thought. He had a very healthy respect for volcanoes, especially sexy-looking ones. "But that only holds for a man, of course." He underscored his comment with a wink.

Ginny stiffened. She didn't like the wink. Liked less what it seemed to do to her. She felt as if she were receiving tiny shock waves being telegraphed through the air. Had to be the empty stomach, she thought. She always fared worse on one, but there just hadn't been time to eat. There never seemed to be enough time anymore, and arguing with this man was eating up a precious supply of it.

She pulled her elbow away. "I demand to see the judge."

Quint took hold of her elbow again, this time more firmly. He knew just how to hold it to keep her in place. "Now we've been all through this, Geneva. The judge is away." He opened the cell and ushered her inside.

The clang as the door shut again seemed to echo in her head. This just couldn't be happening. "Do you intend to keep us here overnight?" she demanded.

"Looks that way." Maybe if Ginny thought she had no choice, Quint mused, she and Jenny would band together instead of be at each other's throats.

She was going to rake this hustler over the coals when she got out of here, Ginny vowed. With or without the law behind her. She fixed him with a no-nonsense look. "My sister and I are *not* going to spend the night in a cell and sleep on a cot."

He'd had already given that some thought. "There might be a way around that."

Ginny's eyes narrowed. With all her heart, she wished she'd taken her tape recorder with her. No matter, her word would have to do. Hers against his. All she had to do was get him somewhere where the phones had keypads on them instead of dials with holes. Until then, she had to be very careful.

"And just what might that be?" Suspicion underlined every syllable.

He exchanged looks with Carly. "You could spend the night at the ranch." It wouldn't be the first time he'd brought home a so-called prisoner, someone needing just a touch of rehabilitation within an understanding atmosphere.

"The ranch," she repeated, staring at him. The least he could do was attempt to be devious. He wasn't even trying.

"The Shady Lady," Quint clarified.

Oh, God, a brothel, Ginny realized with horror. Everything fell into place, crystal clear. This sheriff with the drop-dead smile and long lashes was into white slavery. She wished she had been more explicit in the message she'd left Cliff so he'd know where she was. And then she remembered. The detective she'd hired to find Jenny knew where she was. Cliff could—

Belatedly she realized that Cliff and the detective didn't know one another from Adam. The connection could never be made.

And she and Jenny wouldn't be found until it was too late.

Horrified, Ginny moved her body in front of Jenny's, instinctively trying to shield her. "If you think for one minute that I'm going to let you take my sister to some brothel—"

"Brothel?" Carly scratched his head, completely mystified. "What's she talking about, Quint?"

Broad shoulders rose and fell. "Damned if I know."

He was doing that deliberately, Ginny thought. "Don't play the innocent with me. It won't wash. You're a lot smarter than you let on." And she was on to him.

His smile lazily crept along his lips again. "Nice to know you think so."

Ginny raised her chin. "But I'll kill you before I let you touch my sister."

She'd finally managed to lose him, he thought. "Touch your sister?"

Yeah, right, he didn't know what she was talking about. She really believed that, Ginny thought sarcastically. "You lay one hand on her—just try to get her to that ranch and I'll—I'll—" Lost for a weapon, Ginny pulled her high heel off and held it up like a stiletto knife instead of a stiletto heel. "—I'll hurt you."

She looked adorable, Quint decided, brandishing her shoe as if it was some sort of martial arts weapon. It would take almost no effort on his part to quickly disarm her. For now, he allowed her to clutch the shoe. What was hard was keeping the grin off his face.

"I'm sure you could, but why would you hurt me for taking you to my parents' ranch?"

She looked from the sheriff to the deputy. "Parents' ranch?"

It was worse than Ginny thought. The whole family was in on it.

3

Half-formed thoughts spun around Ginny's head as she tried to find a safe way out of the situation. At all costs, she had to protect her sister. Granted it was two against two and the deputy wasn't quite as broad and strong looking as the sheriff was, but the fact that she and Jenny were standing behind bars definitely tipped the scale in her disfavor.

Ginny mustered the sternest voice she could manage. She was a lawyer and this was the most important argument of her life. She had to win it. Head high, she looked the sheriff straight in the eye.

"You let us go right now, and I won't tell anyone about this incident."

It was a lie. She had every intention of blowing the whistle on this two-bit white slaver, but she couldn't do that if she wasn't free. The first order of business was getting Jenny and herself out of here. The rest would fall into place quickly enough after that.

"What incident?" Quint leaned his shoulder

against the bars, curiosity taking a good toehold. Just what was going on in this woman's mind?

Not for a minute was she about to be taken in by those wide, innocent eyes of his, Ginny thought. Probably had never had an innocent day in his life. He knew exactly what she was talking about. That she was forced to reiterate it only served to further anger her.

"That you arrest innocent young women and then force them to do unspeakable things."

Had to be the fast living, Quint decided. It fried a person's brain if they stayed in the big city long enough. He glanced at his cousin. Carly looked to have even less of a clue than he did.

"I never heard of eating my mother's cooking referred to as an unspeakable thing, have you, Carly?"

Carly winced when he thought of how Aunt Zoe would react to a statement like that. "Nope."

Ginny curled her fingers around her shoe, beginning to feel just the slightest bit uncertain. She lowered the heel a fraction, though her tone remained unchanged.

"Don't play innocent with me—"

For just a split second, Quint's mind hung on the word *play*, spinning a fantasy. Small, tight and complete in the blink of an eye. It had no place here and now.

"I wouldn't dream of it. But speaking of innocent, your sister isn't. She was caught red-handed. And as for you—''

Ginny knew exactly what he thought or supposedly thought he had against her, and they both knew it didn't carry weight. ''None of that warrants being sold into white slavery.''

For one moment, there was only the sound of her words, dying away in the still, late-afternoon air. Quint didn't even think he heard Carly breathing.

Quint's eyes narrowed. ''Now I know things move rather slowly here in Serendipity and maybe we're not the fastest thinkers the country's got, but—what the hell are you talking about, woman?'' Had she completely lost her mind, or were things really so out-of-control where she came from? Just what kind of law enforcement officers did they have wherever she came from? ''I'm offering you a hot meal and a comfortable bed. From the looks of your sister—'' he nodded toward Jenny ''—she could use both.''

Taking offense, Jenny straightened.

''And in exchange for those essentials, we do what?'' Ginny challenged.

''Eat and sleep,'' he replied simply. ''Why, what else would you want to do?''

Momentarily lost, Ginny wasn't sure just what to believe. She let her hand drop to her side. ''Then you're not—?'' She drew a deep breath. The only way to say this was to say it. ''I mean, you don't want to make slaves of us?''

There was no way Quint could keep the amusement from his eyes. He'd held it back as long as he was physically able as it was.

"I make it a policy to keep my fantasies separated from my job, Ginny." He could see the indecision in her eyes. He tipped the scale with his best weapon—logic. "And if I wanted to have my way with you, I certainly wouldn't take you to my parents' ranch. Mrs. Cutler didn't raise any foolish children, Ginny."

He glanced at his watch. It would take them a while to get to the ranch. If they were going to go, they had to leave now.

"Now the choice is yours, but I'd suggest you make it soon because Ma's really strict about how long she'll keep food waiting on the table." Zoe Cutler had the biggest heart in the state, but she thought of herself as a benevolent dictator whose every word was to be obeyed. "Take it from me, you don't want to get on her wrong side."

Ginny didn't care about his mother's wrong side or her right one. As far as she was concerned, any woman who had spawned Sheriff Quint Cutler was not a woman she wanted to meet. "I won't be here long enough to get on any of her sides."

Quint let the words pass without comment. His only response was a smile.

It was worse than a retort, Ginny realized. The expression instantly seeped under her skin, annoying her. At the same time, it seemed to unsettle her, though how and why she couldn't pinpoint. But it did and that was enough to set her off. And worry her.

He unlocked the door, then barred her exit, waiting. "So, what'll it be, Ginny? Yes or no?"

Jenny knew what her response was. She jumped to her feet, crossing to the newly opened door. "I don't care what her answer is," she told him without bothering to glance at her sister. She knew the reproving look by heart. "Mine's yes. Anything to get out of this crummy cell."

Quint nodded, seeing beyond the bravado. His middle brother had gone through a period like this. Thumbing his nose at the world to prove how blasé he was just so no one would know how truly shaky he felt. So had Morgan.

"Smart move. Ma's making a chicken casserole tonight. That's a whole lot better than the diner's specialty of the day," he assured her. Quint stepped out of the way and let the younger girl pass. But his words instantly slowed her pace. "Now I'm putting you on the honor system, Jenny. I'm trusting you not to run off if you give me your word that you won't."

Standing toe-to-toe with him, Jenny opened her mouth, a ready retort on her lips. But the wisecrack failed to materialize. Instead, she could only look up at him. It'd been a while since anyone had professed to trust her. And that he did, without any basis, left her with an odd feeling she didn't quite understand.

Her defiance mellowed just a shade as she lowered her eyes, and mumbled, "Okay."

Quint believed her. In his experience, most people tended to live up or down to the expectations that were placed on them. Jenny deserved a chance to turn around.

"How about you?" Quint turned his attention to Ginny. "Can I trust you?" He raised the handcuffs that hung off his belt. "Or would you rather wear a pair of silver bracelets?"

Ginny's chin rose, though she kept her eyes on the handcuffs. Her chest rose as well, drawing his attention to the fact that she had one of the best figures he'd ever seen.

"What do you think?"

Right now, he figured she really didn't want to know what he actually thought, so he acted as his own censor. "I think that you can be quite a handful when you want to be, Geneva Marlow." He carelessly twirled the handcuffs around his raised index finger. "Question is, do you want to be?"

Ginny didn't like the way he spun the handcuffs around, as if he were just waiting for an excuse to slap them on her wrists. Being handcuffed would definitely complicate things for her. If she read that look in his eyes right, he'd probably wind up handcuffing her to him and then there'd be no chance of escaping.

So she did what she had to do. She put on her shoe and lied again. "I'll behave."

He stepped back and out of her way, holding the door open for her. "Glad to hear that."

Quint didn't believe her for a minute.

The grandfather clock that had been a wedding present from her in-laws over thirty years ago chimed six o'clock just as the front door opened. Zoe Cutler breathed a sigh of relief. Finally.

"Well, it's about time you showed up," she declared as her second son walked in through the door. "The casserole was beginning to turn to stone." She saw that, as promised, Quint had brought company. Zoe loved a full table. "Carly, you're always welcome."

She nodded at her nephew, but her attention was focused on the two women Quint was ushering in before him. Her mother's heart stirred with compassion when she looked at the younger of the two. She was reminded of a bedraggled kitten she'd once saved from drowning in the river.

"Nice of you to join us. I'm Zoe Cutler." Zoe clasped Jenny's hands in both of hers, patting them more than shaking. She did the same with Ginny. Zoe's hands were warm, as was her smile.

A distant, nascent yearning rippled through Ginny as Zoe's hands released hers.

Jenny looked around the large, spacious living room that smacked of Western decor. There was a sense of freedom and spaciousness about the room that seemed to echo and reflect the land upon which it sat. She couldn't quite understand how it could seem cozy at the same time.

It wasn't like any home she'd ever been in.

"Nice place you have here," Jenny murmured half under her breath.

Zoe loved hearing Will's handiwork praised. "The compliment belongs to my son since he was the one who remodeled it."

Ginny looked at Quint in surprise. Though still suspicious of his motives, her initial opinion of him was beginning to shift just a little. "You do remodeling when you're not busy arresting people?"

"Not me, my older brother, Will. He's an architect." Quint dropped his hat on the credenza. "He kept adding on to the house and then had to redo what was originally here." He didn't add that it was a fire that had necessitated the remodeling, a fire that had destroyed half the house and made them all realize how really precious life was. "He built Kent's place, too. That's the house we passed on the way here," he tacked on. He hadn't commented on it, but he'd noticed that she had stared at the ranch-style house as they'd driven by it.

"Kent?" Was the name supposed to mean something to her?

"My brother," Quint clarified. Since Serendipity was such a small town where everyone knew everyone else, he tended to forget that outsiders were not privy to that information.

"Who I'm beginning to think has better manners than you do," Zoe admonished. She gave up waiting. "Quint, you haven't introduced me to your guests."

"We're hardly his 'guests.'" Ginny slanted a look toward Quint. Being in his mother's company kept the word *prisoners* from her lips. So instead, she beat Quint to the punch. "I'm Geneva Marlow." She nodded toward Jenny. "And this is my sister, Jenny."

"Jennifer," Jenny corrected. If Ginny could be Geneva, then she could be formal, too, she thought. Jenny sounded too much like a child anyway, and she was tired of being treated like one.

Though it was almost after the fact, Zoe acknowledged the introductions.

"I'm pleased to make both your acquaintances." Zoe turned toward Quint, trying to gauge just what was going on here. He'd told her all about locking up the sisters and why. What he hadn't made altogether clear was why he wanted to bring them to the ranch, but that would come out in due time, she judged. Until then, she could wait. From what she saw, both young women could do with a little attention and a good meal.

"Hank was going to stay," she told Quint matter-of-factly, "but he wanted to ride on up to Billings to see if he could get Jim Tally to design the wedding rings. Kent decided to go with him. He suddenly realized that with his own wedding following three weeks after Hank's, he'd better get a move on. Wyatt went along to give them both moral support." She didn't add that Hank's best friend had insisted on paying for all the rings as a wedding present to both brothers.

The last Quint had heard, his youngest brother had gone back to his home in Southern California. With the wedding breathing down his neck, maybe he was developing itchy feet. "Hank's here?"

"Was," Zoe corrected. "Came here this morning, tearing through like a twister."

Just like when they were kids. Quint laughed. "Nothing new there."

Hank. Another name. Despite her desire to remain detached from anything that had to do with this man, Ginny found herself trying to keep up. She'd always been competitive to a fault. "Hank?"

He nodded. "My brother."

This man had more brothers than Joseph in the Bible. "Is half the county your brother?"

Rather than take issue at the touch of sarcasm in her voice, Quint laughed.

"Sometimes it felt that way when I was growing up, but I've only got three." He slapped Carly on the back in a gesture that smacked of pure affection. "If you don't count old Carly here who might as well be a brother, he's here so often."

"Don't pay him any mind, Carly." Ginny turned

to see a tall, trim man walking into the room. The resemblance to Quint hit her immediately. Another brother? If he was, she'd bet that he was the oldest of the clan.

Jake Cutler crossed to his nephew as he joined them. "He likes having you around as much as the rest of us do. Maybe more. You're the only one who'll listen when he talks."

The patriarch of the Cutler clan turned his attention to the young women. Zoe had told him that Quint was bringing around two sisters who were temporarily stranded in town. His blue eyes lit appreciatively, the smile on his face making him look almost as young as his sons.

This was the summer of lovely women, he mused. First Brianne Gainsborough had arrived to take pictures of a working ranch and had developed not only magnificent photographs but also a relationship with his son Kent that would last forever. Then Hank had brought Fiona Reilly up from Southern California, dropping the bombshell that he was finally leaving his boots permanently under one bed. If that wasn't enough of a surprise, Denise Cavanaugh had come into town, driving a big rig and carting around carnival rides. One look at her had Will wanting to ride the merry-go-round for the rest of his days. And now these two flowers had been plucked down in their midst. Made a man's head spin. "Hello, I'm Quint's father, Jake Cutler."

"I'm Geneva Marlow, and this is my sister—" Ginny hesitated before saying, "Jennifer."

Following protocol, Jake shook the older one's hand first, then took the younger woman's hand in his. Hardly more than a baby, he thought. Too young for even Carly. The notion made him chuckle under his breath. He'd taken to being a matchmaker in his old age.

"If I'd known that the prisoners were this pretty, I would have run for sheriff myself."

The label should have made her feel uncomfortable, Ginny thought. Instead, she found herself charmed and amused.

Zoe sniffed. Carly tried to bite his tongue and not laugh. "Behave yourself, old man, or I'll hide your vitamins."

Jake lifted a shoulder. Ginny could have sworn there was a definite twinkle in his eyes. "Don't need vitamins, just the right kind of inspiration." He winked broadly at his wife.

Zoe sighed, but there was no missing the affection in her voice.

"Men, they're incorrigible, the lot of them. You can see why I welcome female companionship," she told Jenny. The lines about her mouth softened in the wake of her coaxing smile. "Would you like to help me finish setting the table now that I finally know how many will be sitting at it?"

"Table's not set, yet?" Stepping up behind her, Quint gave his mother an affectionate squeeze.

"Thought you were complaining that we were late."

Zoe absorbed the hug before pretending to bristle and disengaging Quint's arms from about a waist that was still amazingly trim after five children. "Keeps you on your toes—and don't sass your mother, Quintin. Let's go, Jennifer."

Automatically falling into step behind her, Jenny abruptly stopped to look at Quint.

He was surprised that she'd think to ask permission. It convinced Quint that she wasn't a bad seed, just a girl in need of a little straightening out. His hunch was that she even welcomed it. "It's okay."

Ginny watched in amazement as the first hint of what passed for a smile flickered across her sister's lips. Maybe there was a little hope to be had after all.

"That's incredible," Ginny murmured under her breath.

"What is?" Quint asked.

She hadn't realized she'd said it out loud. "My sister doesn't listen to anyone, let alone do things like set the table."

This past year, whenever she was able to be home at a decent hour, she could never get Jenny to do anything for her. The extent of Jenny's participation was to argue with her about everything.

"Ma's got that effect on people," Quint explained, not without a little pride.

What was it like, Ginny wondered, to be proud of your parents instead of ashamed?

"Can I get you something to drink?" Jake offered as his wife disappeared into the kitchen with Jenny. "Soft drink, some wine? I've got beer, but—"

Ginny noted the animated note in his voice as he made the last offer. She preferred wine, but that didn't seem to fit in here. "Beer'll be fine. It's been a while since I had any."

She liked Quint's parents, she decided. They seemed to be everything hers had never been. Warm, in tune to one another. And present. The last counted for a great deal.

Jake nodded his approval of her choice. "I like a woman who can appreciate a good bottle of beer." He rubbed his hands together in anticipation. "Be just a minute." He began to leave the room, then turned to look at his nephew. Since his brother's untimely death twenty years ago, he'd come to look upon Carly as another son. "Carly, why don't you help me bring up a few bottles from the cellar?" He added the kicker, though with Carly, there was no need. The boy was always ready to do anything any of them asked him to do. "Got a fresh batch cooling down there."

"Don't have to ask me twice, Uncle Jake."

Alone with Quint, Ginny felt a restlessness taking hold. At a loss, she began to examine the array of photographs on the mantel. They were of children in various poses, at various ages, all grinning. Boys, mostly, although there was a very striking girl in their midst, her hair blonder than the others. So he had a sister, as well?

The touch of envy returned.

Quint came up behind her as she picked up the group shot that had been taken at the lake last summer. He reached over her shoulder and indicated each individual as he recited their names.

"That's Will, Kent, Hank, you already know me and that beauty's Morgan. You wouldn't know to look at her that she's got a temper that makes snakes shrink back into the skins they've shed once she gets going."

He was close enough for her to feel the tickle of his breath along her neck as he spoke.

"Not at first glance, no," she murmured, shifting aside. Desperate for a moment to regroup, she said, "Your parents seem very nice." Smooth, very smooth, she admonished herself.

If the statement sounded strained, he didn't let on. "You sound surprised." He leaned his elbow against the mantel, studying her. "Were you still expecting me to bring you to some den of iniquity?"

Color rose to her cheeks. "No, I just didn't think of you as having parents, let alone nice ones, that's all."

There was something about the way she said "nice ones" that gave him an inkling of what had been in her past. To spare her, he allowed the focus to remain on him. "Doesn't go with the cloven hoof?"

Arched brows drew together. "What?"

"Well, you have to admit that you kept acting as if you thought I was the devil himself when you first walked into the office."

That was because she thought he was. Now, she wasn't a hundred percent sure. The devil wouldn't bring her to his parents' home. Relenting, Ginny was willing to admit that maybe she had come on a little too strong. But she'd had reasons.

"I was just worried about Jenny, and I didn't know what to think when I heard that she'd been thrown in jail." She sighed, wishing she had the answers. If not all, at least a few. "She's just a young girl."

The concern was genuine, Quint thought. It wasn't hard to see that. That gave them something in common. He'd been worried about his siblings a time or two.

"A troubled young girl."

For a second, she'd forgotten that he was a complete stranger. She wasn't in the habit of sharing personal matters with strangers. Not even good-looking ones.

Ginny straightened her shoulders, as if bracing for a confrontation. "That isn't any of your concern."

He had a different opinion. "It is if she brings her trouble into my town."

His town. Maybe her first impression of him wasn't that far off after all. "Now you sound like some modern-day Wyatt Earp."

He was far from insulted. As a kid, he'd eaten up stories of the Old West. True stories. "Old Wyatt had his virtues. He kept a peaceful town while he wore a badge. That's all I'm after."

It didn't take much to envision him with double holsters strapped to his thighs, slowly making his way down the main street, facing down some desperado. Ginny blotted the image from her mind. She couldn't afford to let herself get carried away.

"And you plan to keep it safe by throwing hardened criminals like my sister in jail."

"And you," Quint couldn't help teasing. "Don't forget you."

All traces of freshly budding camaraderie vanished. "Are you laughing at me?"

His answer surprised her. She expected him to be evasive. Or lie. He didn't.

"Yes. You're taking yourself far too seriously, Ginny." Giving in to impulse, he tested the softness of one of the curls that rioted about her face and shoulders. "The world's not going to stop if you crack a smile once in a while and learn how to kick back. Might do you a whole lot of good, actually."

She jerked her head back out of his reach and

felt her hair pulled for her trouble before Quint could release the strand.

"If I wanted advice on how to live my life, you wouldn't be the person I'd go to."

He wondered if she sought help from some expensive shrink and then decided that she probably wasn't the type. Out here, they had mountains for that. Being out in God's country cleared a man's mind and put his soul in order faster than any expensive psychiatrist.

"Now there, Ginny, you might find that you're missing out."

Neither one realized Zoe had come to fetch them until they heard her huge sigh. They turned almost in unison.

"Are you two going to keep swiping at each other, or are you going to come into the dining room and sit down to dinner like civilized people?"

The dining room was a few short steps away. Quint took them, escorting Ginny by what he guessed was against her will.

"Well, since I have a choice, I'll pick the latter." Quint pulled a chair out for Ginny. "You're a saint, Dad," he declared as his father and Carly, both embracing bottles against their chests, walked into the room. Quint took a bottle of beer for himself and an additional one for Ginny.

"His sainthood is debatable," Zoe informed her son, humor playing along the outline of her lips. "But he is a handy man to have around. Now, before this casserole becomes completely inedible, let's all sit down and have dinner, shall we?'' She looked to her right. ''Geneva, if it's not too much of a hardship for you, take the seat next to Quint. Jennifer,'' she addressed the girl on her right, ''you come sit by me.''

Jenny did as she was told. Taking her seat, she looked up at the older woman.

''It's Jenny,'' Jenny told her quietly. Her eyes remained on the napkin she was spreading on her lap.

''I always liked the name Jenny.'' Zoe passed the mashed potatoes to her left. ''That was going to be Quint's name if he'd turned out to be a girl.''

This was the first Quint had heard of it, but he let it go. He figured his mother had her reasons for coming through with this bit of history.

The information begged for a comment, but Ginny said nothing. She'd barely heard the exchange. She was too busy staring at her sister. It seemed to be almost a miracle. The glazed look of hostility that she'd become so accustomed to had all but faded from Jenny's young face.

4

Pushing away from the dining table, Jake leaned back in his seat, a contented smile on his face.

"One of your best meals, Zoe." There wasn't so much as a trace of the casserole left on his plate. "Hard to believe that was actually healthy for me." He looked around at the faces of the others sitting at his table. "What that woman can do with food is nothing short of a miracle."

Unabashed pride echoed in his voice. It was no secret that he credited his wife with bringing him back to the living after the minor heart attack he'd suffered five years ago. She'd gone out of her way to make sure that the quality of his life only improved, despite the gastronomic restrictions he now adhered to.

Zoe rose from her chair and winked at Jenny. "See? You train them right from the very beginning and then all they need is a little fine-tuning from time to time."

The warm smile the older woman gave her husband told Ginny that what was really fine-tuned here was the relationship between the pair. Envy tugged at her heart again, not just because she envied Quint for the life he must have had, growing up in a warm, loving environment, but because she envied Jake and Zoe for the comfortable happiness they so obviously shared, something she knew had to be very, very rare.

Something she didn't have a prayer of finding. Especially since she wasn't even looking. The hunt was not for her. Not with so many men out there who were like Luke, the man who had temporarily been her stepfather during years she wanted to forget.

Zoe saw the indecision on Jenny's face. The girl needed a little help making an offer. "So, Jenny, are you up for helping an old lady with the dishes?"

Quint hooted at the term. He knew almost better than anyone that nothing kept his mother down. She always had more energy than any of them, except for maybe Morgan and in that case, it was a tie.

"The day you become an old lady is the day the world'll end," Quint told his mother. His reward was the smug smile that creased her lips.

Jake laughed under his breath. "You certainly didn't act like an old lady last night."

Color, as bright as the blush on a red rose, swiftly made a trail up Zoe's neck to her cheeks. She shot him a look that wasn't altogether reproving.

"Hush, old man, we've got company present."

Accustomed to their exchanges, Carly got up, reaching for the emptied casserole dish. "I'll help you clear the table, Aunt Zoe."

But Zoe shook her head. She had plans that didn't include her affable nephew. At least for now. "Thank you, Carly, but I thought I might like a little female companionship tonight. Exclusively." She deliberately shifted her gaze to Jenny.

Jenny shrugged, but to Ginny's eye, the gesture didn't look quite as indifferent as it usually was. "Sure. Why not?"

Feeling awkward by the attention momentarily focused on her, Jenny rose. Mimicking Zoe, she began gathering dishes together.

Taking her cue from the other women, Ginny rose and followed suit. It would do her good to try and move around. She'd eaten far more than she'd intended to, but it had all been so good, from the fresh salad right on through to the peach cobbler dessert. She was surprised that the button on her skirt wasn't straining to pop.

"No, not you, dear." Zoe placed a hand over Ginny's to stop her. "There's such a thing as too many hands in the kitchen."

"Ha! That's not what you used to say." Quint knew his mother very well and figured he knew what she was up to, but he couldn't resist teasing her anyway.

Zoe tossed her still very blond hair, and sniffed.

"A woman's allowed to change her mind. There is something I would like you to do, Geneva."

"Anything." Her own response surprised her. Normally, she would have asked a suspicious "what?" instead. But there was something imminently trustworthy about the couple that made her feel more at ease than she had in an extremely long time.

"Why don't you go and air out my son?" Zoe waved a hand toward the front door. "His mind seems to be a little foggy tonight."

If she didn't know better, she would have said she was being set up. Ginny felt instantly ashamed of herself. These people were too kind and too genial to be considered conniving. It was only that every aspect of her life had been fraught with deception, usually on the parts of people she'd allowed herself to trust.

Like her parents. Like the sheriff in the town she'd come from. The man she'd turned to in her distress, only to discover that he was the worst threat of all.

Quint took her elbow, directing her toward the front and the porch that ran outside. "Looks like we've all been given our assignments for now."

Ginny glanced over her shoulder, but Zoe had already disappeared into the kitchen with Jenny in tow. "She runs everybody?"

He noticed that the question was mildly asked. Her attitude was softening, just as he figured it would. Being around his parents always seemed to bring out the best in people.

Quint nodded in reply, opening the door for her. "Like the queen that she is."

As he closed the door behind him, Quint noted that Carly remained at the table with his father. The two men were each nursing a third bottle of beer. Looked like Carly was staying the night, he mused. Wouldn't be the first time.

Ginny took a deep breath. The air smelled different out here. Clearer, richer. Better.

If she hadn't known better, she would have said that some of the knots in her shoulders were loosening. Leaning against the railing, she looked at Quint. Was all this calculated on his part, or were things just as they seemed?

"Your mother's quite a lady."

The grin was just slightly lopsided. "You'll get no argument from me on that."

She picked up on the key word that covered her life. "What will I get an argument from you on?"

She was far too pretty a woman to constantly be spoiling for a fight, Quint thought. He had an urge to comb the riot of chocolate-colored hair away from her face. An urge to kiss her neck and see if it tasted as sweet, as inviting as it looked.

Quint leaned his elbows and back against the railing, his eyes trained on her. "Who says we have to argue?"

He made it sound like something new, Ginny

thought, instead of the ongoing event since she'd first laid eyes on his sexy broad face. "We've been doing a pretty good job of it so far. And you did throw my sister and me into prison."

"A jail cell," he corrected. "Prison's pretty much of a different matter." A gleam entered his eyes. "As you well know, Counselor. And there was no throwing involved," he reminded her. "Just ushering."

A bit of admiration coaxed a hint of a smile from her. He certainly wasn't as simpleminded as she'd first thought. "You tap-dance well."

Quint knew what she meant and took no offense. "I've had lessons."

She laughed softly. He probably had a great deal of practice, getting his stories straight with all the women whose hearts he broke growing up. Was it the same now? Was he juggling two women while seeing a third? Her father had been that way until he'd finally left once and for all.

"I bet you have." Then, because she'd always been truthful, she added, "You're not at all what I thought you were."

Quint cocked his head, searching her face. He found he couldn't quite read her expression. "Is that a compliment, or should I be reaching for armor?"

It was on the tip of her tongue to ask him what he thought, but that would seem flirtatious somehow. Flirting had never been her style. Just shoot-

ing straight from the hip, that was how she oper-
ated. That meant the truth—every time.

"I thought you were out to milk us for money.
Just a fancy speed trap."

Despite the moonlight, the night made her hair
look darker. Almost black. He wanted to touch it
to examine the color.

"No, no need for that," he said easily. "Serendipity's doing just fine the way it is."

He almost reached out and touched her. What
stopped him was the wary spark he saw entering
her eyes, warning him off. Was that because she
still didn't trust him, or was that because something
else had frightened her, making her leery?

"You always been this suspicious of everyone,
or is that something that just develops after passing
the bar exam?"

He was being flippant, but she didn't feel like
being flippant back. At least, not all the way.
"That's something that comes from life."

The life he'd had had taught him to be patient
with people and wait them out until the best
emerged. So far, he hadn't been disappointed. He
had a hunch that their lives had followed very, very
different paths. "Not always."

"All right," she snapped without meaning to,
"my life."

Surprised he'd gotten her this far, Quint pushed
the envelope a little further. "Tell me about your
life, Geneva."

Ginny was on her guard instantly. What was he trying to get on her? "Why?"

He shrugged, wondering if he'd hit a sensitive nerve, or if she was trying to hide something. "Because I want to know."

That wasn't good enough. "Again—why?"

Quint spoke as if he were attempting to approach a pony that had been mistreated. Despite her fancy clothes and her pricey shoes, he was beginning to think that at bottom, that was what he was dealing with. Someone who had suffered some kind of abuse, be it physical or mental.

"Does there have to be more of a reason for it than that?"

Just because she'd eaten at his parents' table, did he think she was too grateful to push for explanations? Ginny thought. "For me. Things don't happen without reasons, that includes having questions occur to you."

The lady was definitely guilty of overanalyzing, no doubt an offshoot of her chosen profession. "Maybe the reason is just pure curiosity. Maybe I think you need to talk, not just to your sister, but to somebody. Before you explode."

Was it her imagination, or had he somehow moved closer to her in the past few minutes? Ginny wondered. It felt as if he was much too close.

"I'm not about to explode," she insisted heatedly.

The force of her answer made Quint's case.

"Yeah, you are. If ever I met anyone who seemed ready to explode, it's you." If it were anyone else, he'd already be massaging the rigidness right out of her shoulders, but he knew she'd suspect an ulterior motive. "Lady, I'd say they could name the next volcano after you—and it wouldn't do you justice."

The hell with her suspicions, Quint couldn't just stand here, looking at her mimic a military-school cadet. In one movement, because he caught her by surprise, he came up behind her and began massaging her shoulders.

"Person keeps things inside for just so long and then one day they all come busting out, taking pieces of you with it."

Shrugging him off didn't seem to have any effect, Ginny realized. "And you wouldn't want to see that happen."

"Nope."

She tried to turn around, but he wouldn't allow it. And the magic his fingers were weaving *was* erasing some of the rigidity she'd been feeling.

"Why?" Ginny demanded, though not with as much force as she would have liked.

She felt a great deal more delicate than she looked and sounded, Quint realized as he continued massaging. "Might be a tad messy to clean up, and this is my town. You walked into it, that makes you my responsibility."

God, this was heaven. It was all Ginny could do

to keep her mind on the conversation. "And when I walk out of your town?"

"You're on your own again." He paused, then turned her around to face him. "If you want to be."

She could feel her heart jumping in her throat. For sanity's sake, she took a step backward, away from him. "What's that supposed to mean?"

Quint figured that was rather self-explanatory, but in her case, maybe not. "Friends can pick up phones anywhere and talk to friends."

"And you want to be my friend?" For a moment back there, Ginny almost let herself get sucked in, but the night air had cleared her brain. No one makes friends in the spate of a few hours, especially when there was a jail cell involved.

Just like no one could fall in love in that amount of time—no matter how pleasing the man was to look at or seemed. She knew just how damn deceptive appearances could be.

Quint heard the sarcastic edge in her voice and chose to ignore it.

"Why not?" When she said nothing, he moved a little farther into her life by asking, "How long have you been taking care of your sister?"

She hadn't really come right out and said she was taking care of Jenny. "Does it show?"

"You came after her, that's taking care in my book. Your parents alive?" He waited for her to tell him it was none of his business.

Instead, she shook her head.

"Eight," she finally said. He looked at her, looking slightly puzzled when she finally answered his first question. "I've been her legal guardian for eight years."

Quint studied her face. She hardly looked twenty-six, but he knew that some women looked younger than they were, like his almost-sister-in-law. Hank's fiancée, Fiona, looked barely old enough to vote, and she was also twenty-six.

Still, he felt compelled to comment, "You hardly look old enough for that."

Ginny laughed softly to herself. Throwing her head back until her hair brushed against her back, she looked up at the sky. She sought out a cluster of stars. Orion's belt. Seeing it seemed to ground her, the way it had when she was little. A librarian had given her a worn book on astronomy to keep as her own, and she had read it over and over until the pages had to all be taped back in.

She waited for the peace to come. But it didn't, not completely. He was standing much too close. "Oh, but I am. At times I feel a thousand years old."

Quint didn't doubt it. Responsibility could be a very heavy burden if you didn't receive any gratitude in compensation.

"Well, you've held up well for a thousand-year-old lady. Must be that newfangled Super Glue they have." He didn't allow his natural humor to veer him from the course of the conversation. "Have you always had this trouble communicating with Jenny?''

Ginny could deny that she was having any trouble, but what was the point? He'd already heard them. Leaning forward on the railing again, she clasped her hands before her.

"No, not always, we were pretty close once, despite the age difference. I'm nine years older. I was seventeen when my mother finally found her end at the bottom of a bottle.'' That had been the indirect cause, but to Ginny, it was alcohol that had killed her mother. Just as it was alcohol that had driven her father away. He'd preferred the company of a bottle to his wife and daughters, never giving a thought to what would happen to them if he left. Without parents in any sense of the word, Ginny had grown up very quickly. "She was a passenger in the car her boyfriend was driving. They were both drunk out of their minds. I don't think she even felt the impact or knew what was happening.''

The smile on her lips was bitter. "I knew she wouldn't have any regrets about leaving the two of us on our own. She'd never had any regrets doing that when we were younger. She was always out partying. First with my stepfather, then without.'' And despite her mother's ties to him, she'd been nothing if not relieved. It meant no unwanted hands groping for her in the night. "My real father left when I was six. Sometimes my mother would take off, too. When she thought of it, she'd leave us with her friends. And there were foster homes along the way, when she couldn't or wouldn't be bothered with us.''

''It must have been rough on you, being on your own so young.''

She had no idea what to do with sympathy. She wasn't accustomed to hearing it. So she ignored it, not giving in to the desire to absorb it. That would only make her weak, and she couldn't afford to be that for the next five or six decades or so.

''I think I was born being on my own.'' At least it felt that way. ''Jenny and I knocked around foster homes for almost a year and then I turned eighteen and was out of the system.''

Quint saw her jaw harden as she silently relived that time.

''But Jenny still had eight years to face. Eight years of going from place to place, never belonging.'' Or worse, she added silently.

''So you took her in.'' Quint made no effort to hide his admiration. That had to be one hell of a burden to take on at eighteen. Since she was a lawyer, that meant she had to work, go to school and take care of her younger sister on top of that.

For a split second, Ginny fairly beamed as she remembered the triumph of being awarded custody. ''First court battle I ever won. And the most important.'' Her eyes met his, and she realized that she'd gone on far too long. What had been in that beer? She was talking more than she ever did.

"Did you tell her that?"

Restless, she moved away from him as she shrugged. "She knows."

That was the problem, Quint thought. People assumed too much about the other people in their lives.

"Did you tell her?" he asked again, more persistently this time.

The emotion behind the words penetrated. Ginny turned to look at him. "That's a very sensitive question for a man to think of."

Quint had his answer in her evasion. "Haven't you heard? I've got a tender side."

Ginny was beginning to believe that. "Your mother raised you right—" Envy took another little nibble. What was wrong with her tonight? She wasn't behaving like herself at all. "My mother didn't raise me at all."

"Maybe not directly," he allowed.

She looked at him accusingly. "What's that supposed to mean?"

"Well, she made you independent, resilient and, from what I can see, tough."

She wasn't about to stand for her mother getting any credit. Her mother had done what she could to lose them. "Not because she consciously tried."

"No," he agreed, "but the results are the same, anyway."

Her annoyance faded in the face of his expression. Maybe it was the single bottle of beer—although she was accustomed to holding her own when it came to that—because she was feeling unusually magnanimous toward the man who was detaining her and her sister unnecessarily in a town the size of a canceled postage stamp. "Maybe you should look into enrolling in law school. You seem to have the knack for bandying words around."

Quint shook his head at the suggestion. "Too much to memorize. I like keeping a clear head."

Ginny had a hunch there was a great deal going on in that head of his. She sighed, turning away. Clouds had moved in, obscuring the constellation. She wondered if that was an omen.

"So what now?"

"What do you mean?"

"After the dishes are finished?" she prompted, but saw he wasn't quite following her. "Are you taking us off to jail again?"

She was indirectly hinting at his letting them go. Quint thought it might be a little premature for Jenny. Besides, he still had the general-store owner to talk to. He couldn't just release Jenny. Ginny was another matter, but one he wasn't going to mention just yet.

"I thought you could spend the night here." He nodded at the house. "There're a lot of extra bedrooms now that we've all moved out. Nothing my mother likes better than to hear the sound of voices in the morning—as long as they're not arguing, although I suspect that, at times, she gets a little lonesome for those, too.''

So his parents' ranch was what—a way station for lost souls in his book? She didn't know whether to be offended or charmed. In either case, she was mystified.

''Is this the normal way you operate?''

''Different circumstances dictate different actions. Your sister's not a hardened criminal, just someone who's confused and might just go off in the wrong direction if someone doesn't take an interest in her.''

Ginny bristled. This man just couldn't help butting in where he didn't belong, could he? ''Are you saying I don't?''

''I'm saying that maybe she needs to see and hear that once in a while from you. I get the impression that your job keeps you away a lot.''

''My *career*,'' Ginny clarified with gritted teeth, ''keeps food in her stomach and designer clothes on her body.'' She'd worked far too long and hard getting her degree and landing this choice position against huge odds to have it dismissed like that.

''Maybe she doesn't care about designer clothes.''

Who did he think he was, Ginny thought, telling her what was important to Jenny? She knew her sister, not him. ''Yes, she does. Because almost all we could afford until I came to work at the firm were secondhand clothes—something Jenny was very, very embarrassed about. Now she fits right in.''

''Takes more than clothes to feel like you're fitting in. Takes someone who's happy with themselves and their surroundings.''

She wasn't going to get angry, Ginny told herself. If she started yelling at him, his parents would hear and she wasn't going to allow him to embarrass her like that. ''I was wrong, you wouldn't make a lawyer. You sound more like a psychiatrist.''

Quint laughed, wondering if she was trying to get his goat. ''Hey, lawyer, psychiatrist, preacher, bartender—they all come under the same heading. A sheriff's got to be a little of everything.''

She raised a brow at his last choice of occupation. ''Bartender?''

''Sure, a bartender hears things that sometimes even wives don't hear.'' Benjamin, the bartender at the Dewdrop Inn was an old friend of his father's and Quint had been privy to a lot of secondhand stories to support his feelings.

''I would imagine that wives are on the last rung of that food chain you just went through.''

Did she realize how caustic that sounded? He had a feeling she wasn't really as hard as she tried to be. ''Not necessarily.''

If he was trying to be nice on her account, he needn't bother. Ginny had no illusions about the institution of marriage. ''I don't know about that.

Most husbands and wives don't communicate at all.''

"Are you a divorce lawyer?"

"No." She didn't think she could stand to be part of that kind of infighting and bickering. "Just seen a lot of unhappiness in my time."

Quint had no doubts that she had. It seemed a shame. And a waste.

"Well, before I asked a woman to do me the honor of becoming my wife, I'd have to feel that I could tell her anything and not lose her."

He'd used the word *honor,* Ginny noticed. Do him the honor of becoming his wife. When had she heard that last? Honor had ceased to have a place in relationships a long time ago, from what she'd seen.

He was probably full of hot air. She decided to call him on it. "And would the reverse be true?"

"Yes."

She blinked, ready not to believe him yet not quite managing it. "You didn't even hesitate."

He shrugged. "I didn't have to."

Maybe he *was* on the level. "That would make you a very rare man."

Quint thought of his family. "Not where I come from."

"You mean your father." She supposed Jake *was* the exception to the rule.

"To begin with, yes," Quint agreed. He let his instincts take over, moving him closer to Ginny.

"But my brothers feel the same. All three of them are getting married soon and the lot of them feel just the way I do. If you can't talk to your wife, if she's not your best friend, then there's no point in getting married."

"Then I'd say the Cutlers of Montana are very, very special people indeed."

He smiled into her eyes. He liked the way she rolled the word *very* around on her tongue. He had no idea why he thought it was so sensual, but it was.

Beside her now, he ran the tip of his thumb along her bottom lip and could have sworn he saw her eyes grow huge. "That's for you to decide, Geneva."

Unable to help himself any longer, Quint lowered his head and brushed his lips along hers, satisfying a curiosity, an itch he'd had since she'd stormed into his office like a dark-haired hurricane on the loose.

Maybe it wasn't very sherifflike on his part, but he knew it was pure Cutler all the way, and he was a Cutler first and foremost.

Surprise came to her riding a lightning bolt, as did the pleasure. The exquisite pleasure that she surrendered herself to before she ever realized that there perhaps should have been the slightest bit of resistance on her part.

Before she ever realized that there was even an encounter.

5

Ginny sighed as his mouth moved slowly, patiently, coaxingly over hers. She felt as if she was falling into a fiery bale of cotton and being consumed by it—and not doing a damn thing about saving herself.

She didn't want to save herself; she wanted to go on enjoying this forever.

Uh-oh.

The two small syllables beat like a prophetic tattoo over and over again in Quint's head. It was that part of his anatomy that he was in over. In over his head. Way over.

Kissing this woman wasn't what he expected, and as the seconds ticked away into eternity, he ceased knowing exactly what it was that he *had* expected, only that this was not it. This was far more pleasurable and dramatic.

Ginny could swear that her heart was going to pop right out of her chest. It was beating so hard and so fast, she couldn't seem to pull her thoughts together and draw them into a coherent whole. All she could think about was his mouth and what it was doing to her, stirring feelings that she had thought had long since atrophied, or at the very least, gone into hibernation.

Hands braced on his shoulders—his oh-so-strong shoulders—Ginny finally forced herself to push him back and create a space between their lips. A space that most of her really didn't want.

But the voice of sanity ordered its existence. It was a voice she had paid attention to all of her life. Obeying it was what had seen her through all the oppressively difficult times of her life.

This was the first time a sense of rebellion accompanied her obedience.

It took her a moment to trust her vocal cords to vibrate. Taking a deep breath, she blew it out again slowly, her dazed eyes fixed on his.

"What was that?"

He liked holding her, Quint thought. Liked resting his hands on the slight, gentle swell of her hips. Liked the way she looked at him without meaning to. As if she felt as dazed as he did right now.

Quint grinned. "If you have to ask, you've been even busier than I thought you were." Then, before she could offer a retort, he elaborated. "That was a kiss on a moonlit porch shared between a small-town sheriff and a sophisticated, stressed-out, lovely lady lawyer."

The man certainly had a way with words, Ginny thought. And a way with his lips.

Still under the influence, she felt herself smiling even though she knew she should at least attempt to appear annoyed. This shouldn't have happened—should it? No, of course not. But remembering that when her lips were still tingling wasn't easy.

"Details." He described what had just happened with details. Another man would have just said they'd kissed, not dressed the deed in flowery words. "You really should have been a lawyer."

Quint spread his hands in mock humility. "I am what I am."

His tone was deceptively light and deliberately so, covering the mild confusion that he was still experiencing. Kissing Ginny had been more than pleasant, more than nice. Ever so much more. It had been stirring in a way he didn't recall being stirred.

This bore, he knew, further exploring. Under the right circumstances.

Ginny had taken in several deep breaths and her mind was no closer to being cleared than before. And she knew why. It was because he was still standing too close. She had a feeling that perhaps if he stood in Seattle, she might have a chance.

Believing that her best defense was a strong offense, she tried to go on the attack.

"Isn't there some conflict of interest here, the sheriff kissing his prisoner?"

Quint saw the change and said nothing. "Well, you're not exactly a prisoner, and at any rate, you wouldn't have been mine, but the town's."

"Not exactly a prisoner?" Ginny repeated. Now what was he trying to pull? "Then what am I—?"

She fixed him with a demanding look, willing him to explain.

The look in his eyes, sensual and amused, told her that she'd blundered in her phrasing. "I've got a hunch that that would probably take me the better part of the night to tell you."

Quint saw the flash of annoyance reappear in response, but it didn't have nearly as sharp an edge to it as before. The kiss had affected both of them, he realized with a touch of relief. Nice to know the lady wasn't as cool and aloof as she pretended to be. But then, he hadn't really thought she was.

"But the short of it is that you're not a prisoner," he told her only to see her mouth drop open in speechless surprise. He noticed that for once suspicion hadn't accompanied the look. "I've decided to drop the charge against you. I can understand how your extreme concern for Jenny's safety might have caused you to talk to me the way you did."

Flabbergasted at the new twist in the events, Ginny didn't know whether to take a swing at Quint for stringing her along like some idiot when he had undoubtedly meant to drop the charge all along— or kiss him because every fiber of her body wanted her to.

Struggling, she opted for a toned-down version of the former. "I don't understand. Why did you bring Jenny and me here if we were free to leave?"

She still didn't get it, did she? Quint thought. "Oh, but you weren't and you're not. At least Jenny isn't free to leave yet and I figured that you'd want to stick around to help her."

Just what else was he "figuring"? Suspicion took hold again. Just because the man's kiss could melt her pantyhose clean off didn't mean she had to trust him. Quite the opposite. "Is this more of the same game?"

Had he had Morgan's temper, Quint might have resented the implication. But he was more like Will and let the words and accusation roll right off his back.

He leaned a hip against the railing, arms folded before him as he regarded her. "The only kind of games I play involve a deck of cards. Jenny shoplifted and there's another party involved in this besides her and the law she broke."

They'd danced this dance before. "The general-store owner."

Quint inclined his head in agreement. "The general-store owner."

In all likelihood, Quint figured it wouldn't be difficult to prevail on Joe not to press the charges against the young girl. Joe had a granddaughter just about the same age and that tended to soften a man to the situation.

But letting her go wouldn't really help Jenny in the larger scheme of things. Though she didn't admit it, he had a feeling that Ginny agreed with him.

Ginny chewed on the inside of her lip, an unconscious habit she'd always had when she circled a problem. "Maybe if I spoke to him—"

Quint tried not to stare at her mouth. Discovering that it could be sweet and stirring as well as sharp didn't help his powers of concentration any. "If you're going to speak to anyone, I suggest you start with Jenny and make that speak with, not to."

"I have, and you heard the results." Ginny knew he'd overheard them arguing. Talking to Jenny was like trying to talk to a wall and get a response.

"Like I said, with, not to."

Her back went up, her eyes narrowed. Was this another criticism? "Meaning?"

"No one likes a lecture." Quint saw the look in her eyes and tried not to laugh. Only a smile creased his mouth. "As you can readily testify first-hand."

Damn, but he had a smile that sliced right through her. Ginny wanted to be angry at him, not moved by him. And least of all, she didn't want to react to him physically. So far, she wasn't faring very well.

Her smile was almost rueful as she told him, "You're making it awfully difficult for me to make up my mind about you."

His smile only went further in unsettling her. "Good, a little mystery is always a good thing between a man and a woman."

She looked at him sharply. Was he implying that

something was going to happen between them? That he thought she'd go to bed with him just because she wanted to free her sister? "When did we become a man and a woman?"

"Why, I think nature took care of that right from the beginning."

Ginny didn't know whether to be embarrassed at her assumption or annoyed that he had set her straight for the mistake. She couldn't tell if he was laughing at her or not. She chose to ignore it and plowed to the heart of the reason they were here.

"So what happens to Jenny? Does she sit in jail until the judge comes back from wherever he is?" She couldn't believe that Quint would do that to her. If nothing else, his mother wouldn't let him.

"Well," he drawled, deliberately playing the hayseed he knew she still believed him to be. "I have the authority to release her on her own good behavior if I wanted to—"

Thank God. "Great—" Ginny turned, ready to reach for the front door. They could be on their way within the hour.

He moved to block her way. "Except that she hasn't proven that she has any good behavior, at least, not in large supply."

Frustrated, Ginny thought she was going to scream. She glared at Quint. "Are you deliberately trying to drive me crazy?"

He fixed her with a long, steady look. "No, you'll know when I deliberately try to do that." The wink sent tidal waves rippling through her system. Ginny felt as if she had just been put on notice. Of what, she couldn't put into words. But it definitely made her feel antsy.

"So what are you saying—exactly?" Antsy or not, she wasn't about to let him tap-dance his way out of this until she had a straight answer.

"I might be able to sway Mr. Taylor if Jenny offers restitution." That had been Quint's plan all along, ever since he'd put Jenny into the cell to cool off. Having Ginny remain was just a bonus.

Restitution. So it was about money after all. The prick of disappointment seemed even sharper than she'd counted on. Ginny squared her shoulders.

"How much?"

She still thought in terms of money, Quint realized. He shook his head. That came from having a great deal—or none to start with. He'd already figured out that it was the latter with her.

"Not how much, what kind."

"Excuse me?"

"Mr. Taylor's assistant just went off to college." The summer was only half over, but Taylor had told him Ruby'd made up her mind to go. "It's early," he allowed, seeing the dubious look on her face. "But Ruby wanted to settle in, so that leaves him really shorthanded. I figure Jenny could work off her debt to him by helping out in the store." He considered a reasonable time frame. "Say, ten days' worth?"

Ginny's brows rose high, completely disappearing beneath her bangs. "For a package of cupcakes?"

"Several packages," he reminded her. But there was more at stake here than that and she knew it. "And it's not the amount but the crime itself. Ever read *Les Misérables?* The main character was hounded to his grave because he stole a loaf of bread to feed his hungry daughter."

She figured that if there were any feathers in the vicinity, they could have been used to knock her over. "You read *Les Misérables?*"

Quint got a kick out of the amazement in her eyes. He'd wager that she probably had no idea she was prejudiced. "Twice, why?"

Ginny shook her head, feeling just the slightest bit embarrassed for what she'd been thinking about his mental abilities. The man was full of surprises.

"Nothing, you didn't seem the type to read anything but…"

"Men's magazines?" he suggested when her voice trailed off.

That was exactly what she'd been thinking, but she knew when to gracefully withdraw. "I think I'd better stop right here."

He grinned. "Good idea."

Somewhere in the distance, crickets were serenading one another, searching for their soul mate. The air was alive with their music. She'd forgotten what that sounded like, she realized. Then it had been nothing but annoying to her, now it was almost soothing.

She turned to face him, ready to deal.

"All right, suppose I let my sister be sold into servitude for ten days. Just what am I supposed to do in that time? I can't go back and forth to Southern California." He probably had this all figured out, too. Part sheriff, part philosopher, part con artist. A modern renaissance man, she thought, a hint of amusement curving her mouth.

Quint wondered what caused her smile, but addressed her question instead.

"Well, actually you could, but it would be time-consuming and a waste for everyone all around." He included himself in that reckoning. "Your other option is to stick around for the ten days and give your sister the moral support and encouragement she needs."

Ginny really wished he'd stop telling her what her sister needed, as if she were the outsider in this instead of him. "The town have a hotel?"

Quint thought of the old building where he'd worked after school to earn a little extra money of his own. It stood two stories and if its rooms were half-filled, they were doing well.

"We do, but it's closed for repairs."

Which in this case might have meant that they were changing the light bulb, Ginny thought. She didn't recall seeing any large buildings in town when she'd come looking for Jenny.

"Figures."

"My folks'll be glad to put you up for more than the night." If he knew his mother, she'd insist on it, which was a lucky thing because the other alternative was to remain in the cell at night.

"You're awfully free with their hospitality. Shouldn't you ask first?"

She obviously had no working knowledge of Western hospitality or close-knit families. "Don't have to. My mother loves taking in people, and she's already taken a shine to your sister."

Taking in people. The term rankled. The year before she turned eighteen, she and Jenny were always being taken in. Always treated as something a little less than human. Her chin rose.

"We're not poor strays."

The lady had a lot of extra baggage she was carrying around with her. "Not that I used the term, but a person doesn't have to be poor to be a stray. It's a matter of how you feel inside that decides it."

He was uncomfortably close to the truth, Ginny realized. "Do you always spout philosophies like that?"

The look on Quint's face was genial. "Only if the situation warrants it."

They heard the sound of the door opening behind them. Ginny turned to see Jake poking his head out. There was an apologetic expression on his face.

Nodding at Ginny, his eyes shifted toward his

son. "Don't mean to be interrupting anything, but your mother sent me out."

Quint straightened. "You're not interrupting anything, Dad. I'm just talking Geneva into staying at the Shady Lady until Jenny's slate is wiped clean."

Ginny expected to see a look of protest on the older man's face. None appeared.

Jake grinned. Again Ginny was struck by the similarity between father and son.

"That's what she sent me out to ask, but as usual, you're way ahead of me, Quint." He looked at Ginny. "So, did he twist your arm too hard?"

Obviously he was acquainted with the way his son browbeat people. Suppressing a smile that seemed to materialize naturally around the older Cutlers, Ginny shook her head. "Not too hard."

"Glad to hear it." Not that he'd had any doubts. Hank might be the golden-tongued one in the family, but Quint was none too shabby in that department. Jake had no doubts that his second son could talk a snake into keeping its skin on an extra season. "I'll help Zoe make up one of the extra bedrooms." He gestured toward them. "Go back to doing what you were doing."

Acting far more pleased than the situation warranted in her estimation, Jake withdrew.

It wasn't until after the door closed that she realized she hadn't told him that she'd agreed to anything. "He really didn't ask if I was staying."

"He didn't have to." His father was good at reading people. Quint had gotten the knack from him. "You would have said no flat out if you weren't."

Ginny baited him. "And if I did now?" He surprised her by shrugging.

"Choice is yours, of course, but personally, I don't think a job—or a career—" he tacked on before she could correct him "—is worth it, not if it means losing touch with people we love. Or worse, losing those people."

Ginny frowned. She hated being backed into a corner. Even more, she hated the fact that this small-town sheriff with his wicked, wicked mouth was absolutely right. If the situation hadn't involved her so directly, if she'd been removed, it would have been exactly what she would have said. Being stuck in the middle put a different spin on it, but at bottom, he was right.

Damn him.

Resigned, she conceded. "We'll stay."

He slipped his arm around her shoulders, not like a man with a woman but like one friend with another. Ginny wasn't certain if she preferred that or not. The man was definitely scrambling her brain.

"Knew you'd come through."

It wasn't so much a matter of coming through as not really having much choice. Quint was right about Jenny. Somewhere along the line she and her sister had lost that closeness they'd had, that interdependence that came of feeling it was them against the world. If they were to remain close—if Jenny was to leave the self-destructive path she was on— Ginny knew she had to cut through the hostility in her sister's soul.

And it looked as if Quint Cutler's way of doing it just might be the key she was looking for.

Not that she'd ever tell him.

Wearing the nightgown that Zoe had loaned her, Ginny leaned over the double bed and fluffed up her pillow. "The Cutlers are nice people."

Jenny had elected to sleep in her camisole and underwear. She sat on the edge of the bed, not quite a prisoner, not quite free. She shrugged indifferently. "They're okay."

Ginny reached for Jenny's pillow and fluffed it as well. "You seemed to think Mrs. Cutler was more than 'okay.'"

Jenny turned, ready for a fight. "What's that supposed to mean?"

Ginny tossed her pillow back into place. Why was there always that hostile look in Jenny's eyes? Why couldn't they just talk? "Only that you seemed to take to her. And she certainly took to you."

Jenny swung her long legs under the covers. "Jealous?"

Ginny bristled at the suggestion. "No, of course not." Quint's words about communicating played themselves through her head. She swallowed her pride. "Yes."

The admission surprised Jenny and she stared at her sister.

"What?"

It wasn't easy opening her feelings to an audience that had been far from receptive for more months than she cared to remember, but there was a great deal at stake. Ginny pushed forward.

"Yes, maybe I am a little jealous. Jealous that you can relate to a total stranger so easily when you can't even talk to me."

Jenny reacted the way she had for the past couple of years. She took Ginny's confession as a criticism against her. "Maybe it's because the total stranger doesn't judge me."

Ginny could feel the conversation slipping away again, out of her control. "I never judge you."

Jenny's brown eyes grew into small, accusing slits. "Yeah, right."

Ginny opened her mouth, ready to vehemently deny the charge, then stopped herself. The sound of raised voices arguing was no way to repay the Cutlers for their generosity. Besides, what good would it do? The harder she tried, the less Jenny listened. Ginny did what she seldom did in life. She temporarily gave up.

With a sigh, she lay down on her side. "You'd better get some sleep, you've got to get up early tomorrow to work in Taylor's store."

Jenny groaned, grumbling under her breath as she tossed herself down on the pillow, her back to Ginny. She didn't want to think about what she had to face tomorrow.

They were sharing a bed, just the way they used to years ago when they were younger, except that now at least it was a double bed instead of a single one.

They'd seemed to come almost full circle, Ginny realized. Who would have ever thought that success brought so much dissatisfaction with it?

Ginny sighed again. Back then, she thought all they needed to solve their problems was each other and a wheelbarrow full of money. Talk about being naive...

"Sheriff going to drive me in tomorrow?"

Ginny turned her head toward Jenny. "Us," she corrected, wanting there to be no mistake that she was here for her. "Drive 'us' in, and yes, he is."

Quint was staying at the ranch tonight instead of driving to town and then back again in the morning. He was putting himself out an awful lot for people he hardly knew. She couldn't shake the feeling of waiting for the other shoe to drop. People just didn't care about other people like this, not without a reason. Not even in postage-stamp-sized towns.

"You know, he's kind of nice, even if he did throw me into jail," Jenny murmured, her voice thick with exhaustion. Sleepiness made her words sound slurred.

"Kind of," Ginny echoed.

Because it was late and she needed to get to sleep, Ginny resolved not to think about Quint Cutler any more that night.

She failed.

6

Ginny looked down at Jenny on the bed. Asleep, Jenny looked the way she always thought of her sister in her heart.

Sweet, innocent.

Ginny savored the impression, knowing it would disappear the moment Jenny opened her eyes and her mouth. But it was getting late, at least by Serendipity's standards. Behind her, dawn was just beginning to unfurl, sending long probing fingers of muted sunlight tapping along the windowpane. Time to get rolling. Taking a deep breath, she cut short her indulgence.

Bracing herself for the heated reception ahead of her, Ginny leaned over the bed and gently shook her sister's arm. Jenny finally responded with a barely audible, completely garbled noise that sounded very much like a growl.

"Jenny, wake up." Ginny gave her shoulder one last shake. "You've got to go to work for Mr. Taylor this morning."

Digging her face out of the confines of her pillow, Jenny rolled over on her back. She raised her head just enough to glance out the window. With a huge sigh, she let her head drop back on the pillow.

"You have got to be kidding me."

Jenny stared at Ginny with eyes that were hardly larger than slits. Somehow, she still managed to telegraph hostility with them.

"No, it's time to get up." Ginny had already hurried into her clothes after taking what amounted to a three-minute shower. Never having had the luxury of dawdling when she was growing up since there'd always been so much to do, Ginny wouldn't have known how to take her time pampering herself even if she'd wanted to.

Turning around, she saw that Jenny had made no effort to move so much as a muscle.

"C'mon," she urged. "I don't like this any more than you do but if we're going to get you out of here, we have to play by their rules."

The small, dismissive snort spoke volumes. "Why can't we just run away—at a decent hour?"

Saying that, Jenny rolled over and pulled the covers up over her head.

Ginny really didn't want to get into an argument first thing in the morning. Biting back a few choice words about Jenny's laziness, Ginny pulled the covers off, depositing them at the foot of the bed.

Yelping in protest, Jenny made a grab for the covers, but Ginny snatched them away before she could reach them.

"Because we have to play by the rules," Ginny told her tersely, "not break them, that's why." What was wrong with Jenny? Why was she so determined to be perverse? "Haven't you learned that running away doesn't solve anything?"

Rather than comment, Jenny tried to cover her head with the pillow. Ginny dragged that away from her, too.

Jenny glared up at her, frustrated and finally wide awake. "I guess not. I couldn't seem to run away from you."

The remark drew blood, just as Ginny knew Jenny had intended. Ginny refused to show her that she'd made a direct hit. Annoyance colored her words. "Just get your butt out of bed and downstairs before someone comes up here and gets it out of bed for you."

The threat didn't produce the desired results. A smile that was half smirk curved Jenny's young mouth. "Wouldn't mind if it was Quint. Or maybe that deputy of his, what's-his-name."

Ginny folded her arms before her, waiting for Jenny to get up. "Carly."

"Yeah." The smirk softened a little. "Carly."

The smile bothered Ginny far more than the remark did. Her sister was growing up a lot faster than she was happy about. Was that her fault, too? Was it all her fault? Had she somehow failed Jenny while she'd been trying so hard to make everything right for her, to give her the things that she herself had never had? The guilt and confusion were tearing her apart.

Ginny picked up the pillow from the floor and tossed it back on the bed, her eyes daring Jenny to reach for it. "More than likely, it'll be Mrs. Cutler coming up to get you, and I don't think you want to show her how pigheaded you are, especially after the way she treated you last night."

Jenny sat up, pulling her knees to her chest. She dragged her hand through her hair.

"Pigheaded," she echoed with a disparaging frown. "That means I'd fit right in here."

No, she didn't fit right in here. With her attitude, the only place Jenny fit in was amid misfits and troublemakers. Ginny would die before she let her exist in a place like that.

For just a moment, she found herself wishing that whatever it was Quint had in mind for Jenny would work before he washed his hands of her, disgusted by Jenny's chip-on-her-shoulder attitude.

"Just keep that smart mouth of yours closed around here, all right?" she warned Jenny. "These are nice people."

Jenny eyed her clothes, thinking of the day ahead. The old man in the store would probably work her until she dropped. He looked the type. "Nice people don't condone slavery."

Jenny had developed a knack of turning things around, of always making it seem as if she were the innocent, put-upon victim, Ginny thought. The only thing Jenny was a victim of was her own nasty disposition.

Ginny fixed her with a look. "Nice people don't shoplift."

The dark eyes shot daggers back at her. "I was hungry!"

Excuses, always excuses. "You wouldn't have been if you'd stayed home where you belong."

Jenny finally scrambled out of bed. On her knees, arms rebelliously crossed before her chest, Jenny glared at her. "How would you know where I belong? You don't know anything about me anymore."

They were back to that again. All they seemed to do was go round and round the same subject. Jenny seemed bent on making her feel as if everything was her fault. Ginny refused to let Jenny see that she'd succeeded in making her feel guilty again, but it wasn't easy keeping the emotions from her face.

She pressed her lips together. "Just get ready, all right?"

It took all she could do not to slam the door in her wake as she left. But a temper tantrum wouldn't solve anything.

It wouldn't even make her feel better.

She made her way downstairs, feeling less than human, less than friendly.

How had she gotten to this state in life? Working

twelve-hour days, no social life to speak of and for what? For a sister who hated her?

A wave of utter defeat tried to work its way through her as her foot met the bottom of the stairs. Ginny fought it off.

There was a light pooling along the floor, coming from the end of the hall. Someone was in the kitchen.

Like a nearly frozen puppy drawn to the warmth of a roaring fire, Ginny was drawn to the warm aroma of freshly brewed coffee coming from the kitchen.

Mrs. Cutler was up early, she mused. She wondered if this was the woman's usual hour, or if having them here had intruded on her schedule.

Ginny stopped short in the doorway. It was Quint, not Zoe in the kitchen. Because his back was to her, she paused a moment to watch him, half in disbelief, half in fascination.

First thing in the morning, and the man looked wide-awake and ready to take on the world. Had to be the air out here, she thought.

He was humming a tune she didn't recognize under his breath and was doing something at the stove. Unconsciously, her eyes swept along his tall frame, lingering at the way his worn jeans fit his hips and neatly hugged his butt.

Probably not an ounce of fat on him and she'd be willing to bet the man had no idea what the inside of a fitness gym looked like.

She thought of the way he'd kissed her last night. Even now, the memory brought a fresh ripple of excitement to her.

Why hadn't some woman made off with him by now?

The answer was simple. He was probably having too good a time to get serious.

Ginny decided that it was best if she weren't alone with him just yet. Maybe she'd see about hurrying Jenny along.

About to retreat, she heard Quint offer a cheery, "'Morning," without even turning around.

Ginny stared at the back of his head. She hadn't made any noise. "How did you know I was here?"

Quint turned around, two cups of coffee, hot and black, in his hands. Crossing to the table, he held one out toward her. Almost reluctantly she came into the room and accepted the offering.

The smile he gave her warmed her more than the sides of the steaming cup she grasped.

"I could say I had eyes in the back of my head, but truth is, I saw your reflection in the glass oven door." He nodded his head toward the wide range behind him. Straddling the kitchen chair, he lowered himself into it and motioned for her to follow suit. When she sat down, he asked amiably, "Did you sleep well?"

So, they were going to engage in neutral conversation over their coffee. She could handle that. Ginny relaxed a little. "Better than I thought."

Quint took a long sip, savoring the dark brew. He liked muscle in his coffee. "Why's that? Can't sleep in strange places?"

She wondered if she looked tired, then wondered why that should matter to her. She wasn't out to dazzle him, just to get this over with.

"Not usually."

The soft laugh curled through her like hypnotic smoke. "Me, I've never had that problem. Hank always said I could sleep in a closet, hanging from a hook. Ma says it's the sleep of an honest man with a clear conscience."

Her look sharpened. "Meaning what?"

She was getting her back up again, Quint thought. It had taken all of ten seconds. Had to be a record, somewhere. He kept his voice low, amiable, the way he would if he were trying to tame a wild animal and make it into a pet.

"Meaning I have a clear conscience, nothing else." He leaned forward, cup in both hands, his eyes on her face. "Geneva, if you don't mind my saying so, you've really got to get over thinking everything has some sort of hidden meaning behind it. Sometimes an acorn is just an acorn—"

Not with her luck lately. "Instead of a miniature bomb?"

He laughed, downing more of his coffee. He was beginning to feel fortified. "You have turned being suspicious into an art form, haven't you?"

Ginny shrugged, feeling self-conscious, yet for

some reason, feeling oddly at ease at the same time. She tried to enjoy it instead of dismantling it for further examination. "Maybe."

There was no maybe about it, Quint thought. The lady was going to wear herself out before she reached thirty, and that would be a powerful waste of a natural resource. "Learn to relax, you'll live longer."

Ginny thought back to her days in Smoke Tree, to the life-style there. She couldn't wait to get out. "It's not longer, it just seems that way."

That sounded oddly like the voice of experience. Quint laughed, shrugging.

"Either way—" He let his voice trail off, leaving it up to her to finish the thought.

Draining the last of his coffee, he glanced at his watch and then at the door. "Where's your sister?" He would have thought the two of them would have come down together.

"Still upstairs, I guess." She hoped Jenny hadn't gone back to sleep. "I woke her up and told her to get ready just before I came down."

That being the case, he'd give the girl a few more minutes before he went up and knocked on the door. Quint rose again, taking his empty cup to the counter. This morning, he needed a second cup to get rolling.

"She'd better hustle if she wants a decent breakfast before we leave."

Ginny looked around, still surprised that she didn't see Zoe. "Where's your mother?"

Quint took out a large pan and placed it on the burner. "I told her to sleep in this morning, that I'd take care of breakfast."

"You?"

The disbelief in her voice nearly made him laugh out loud. "What's the matter, don't men cook breakfast in your world?"

He took out a carton of eggs with one hand, a plate of ham that had already been sliced with the other. Quint used his hip to close the door. Scrambled eggs and fried ham all around seemed simplest.

Ginny couldn't picture him doing anything as domestic as cooking. She had an easier time envisioning him slaying game and dragging it to the table. He seemed far too physical a man to cook.

"Men open boxes of cereal in my world—sometimes badly when they get frustrated."

The remark had him turning to look at her. How many lovers had she had and why hadn't she struck a match to one of them long enough to get a ring out of it? Was it by choice? Was she as discerning as he was, or was there another reason she was single?

"Does that happen often, Ginny? Do men get frustrated around you?"

She knew what he meant. The question was far too personal and hit far too close to home. She wasn't an iceberg, she just hadn't been able to open herself up for a relationship. She'd always been too afraid of being hurt. Of ending up the way her mother had been. Always at the mercy of some man, always looking for a way to anesthetize the hurt.

She drew herself up. "What does that have to do with Jenny?"

The look in his eyes went right through her, stripping her of bravado. She felt as if there was no way she could lie to him, that somehow he'd know. Which was ridiculous.

"Not a thing."

The back door slammed shut, shattering the pregnant moment. It was followed by a very indignant squeal of protest that sounded too much like Jenny not to be. Ginny could feel her heart sinking. Now what?

Quint exchanged looks with Ginny before abandoning breakfast to investigate the source of the noise. He was spared the trouble.

The next moment, Carly walked in, bearing a wiggling, cursing Jenny slung over his broad shoulder, fireman-style. He seemed oblivious to the names she was heaping on his head and what she was saying about his ancestry.

Ginny wasn't and she was mortified.

Carly grinned affably, nodding a greeting at Ginny before reporting to Quint. "Look what I found sneaking out to the barn.'' He turned around so that Jenny could face his cousin.

Quint'd had a hunch that she might try to get away. That was why he and Carly had taken turns staying awake and standing guard outside.

"So, decided to broaden your résumé by turning to horse stealing?'' Quint asked. The girl's cheeks were crimson with indignation. She was going to be something else when she got to be Ginny's age, he judged. If she lived that long. "Put her down, Carly.''

Carly did as he was told. Jenny looked furious enough to spit.

"I wasn't going to steal him. I was going to borrow him,'' she cried heatedly. "But this Neanderthal grabbed me from behind and dragged me over here before I could explain.''

Chagrined and furious at this slap-in-the-face her sister had delivered to their hosts, Ginny was torn between her natural instincts to come to her aid and her sense of justice. The latter dictated that she join the other side.

She did.

"I don't believe you did that. What were you thinking?'' she demanded, confronting Jenny. Jenny refused to look at her. "You can't even ride.''

Jenny set her mouth bitterly. "He does it.'' She jerked an accusing thumb at Carly. "How hard can it be?''

Though his smile was still in place, the look in Quint's eyes was dead-on and stern. This was not, he thought, going to be as easy as he would have liked. That just told him that Ginny needed help with this handful she was trying to raise.

"Put in a couple of solid days at the store helping Taylor, and I'll give you a riding lesson so that you can see for yourself how hard—or easy—it can be. Now sit down and behave yourself. Breakfast'll be ready in a few minutes."

Annoyed, embarrassed, Jenny did as she was told. But to show she wasn't really being submissive, she fixed a sullen stare on the place setting.

"I want to apologize." Feeling awkward, Ginny forced herself to turn toward Quint in the car as she tendered the words.

It had been more than two hours since the incident in the morning. They had just left Jenny with Joe Taylor at the general store. The old man had her stocking the shelves with a fresh delivery of canned goods. Carly had opted to hang around for a bit in case Jenny had any ideas about repeating her early-morning performance.

Harboring the same concerns, Ginny was silently grateful to him.

"About what?" Quint guided his car toward the sheriff's office. A telltale squeal accompanied a right turn. The car was going to have to go in for work soon, he mused.

Ginny lowered her eyes to the dashboard. This wasn't easy for her. She'd long since given up making apologies for anything, least of all her family.

"About Jenny trying to steal your horse." She blew out a breath. There was no sense in holding back. All in all, he'd been pretty nice about this whole thing. "About Jenny, in general."

Quint didn't want her squirming uncomfortably, so he let her off the hook quickly. "Your sister's a good kid. She's just angry, that's all."

Ginny appreciated the comment, but in a way, it made it that much harder for her. Had Quint been critical of Jenny, she could have rallied to Jenny's defense. That he was understanding forced her to be negative—and truthful. "That's no excuse."

"No, it isn't," he agreed, "but it does give us something to work with, something to try to fix." He pulled the car into a space right behind the single-story building.

"Us?" Had she missed something? Since when had they actively joined forces in this?

He flashed a grin. The lady certainly was touchy about help. "Figure of speech generally, but in this case, since you're here—"

Ginny'd always been leery of people volunteering to take over. They usually tried to assume control and she wasn't about to relinquish that to anyone, even a well-meaning, good-looking country sheriff. "And Jenny's my problem—"

Quint glided over her words as if he hadn't heard

them. "And this is my town, I figure that qualifies you and me as an 'us.'"

She had other ideas on the matter. To begin with, he made it much too simple. If it were that easy, she would have been able to set things straight a long time ago, when she first noticed the change in Jenny.

"And you think by making her work at the general store for a week, that'll fix everything."

Quint would have had to have been deaf to have missed the sarcasm in her voice.

"Ten days," he corrected mildly. "And no, it won't fix everything, but it's a start and that's what we need." Before she could protest that all-encompassing word, he added, "I've got other thoughts on this."

The leeriness returned, but it wasn't nearly as all-consuming as it had been. Just why did he take this on as his own crusade? Ginny wondered. There had to be more to it than what he was saying, but for the life of her, she couldn't figure out what. No one had ever put themselves out for her or Jenny. Not even her mother's family. They'd been all too happy to wash their hands of them, and here was this stranger who wanted to help her bring Jenny back into the fold. What was in it for him?

"Such as?"

Quint pulled up on the hand brake and got out of the car. "Ever see *Captains Courageous?*"

Rounding the hood, he managed to open the passenger door for Ginny before she had a chance to.

Getting out, Ginny shook her head. "No, never heard of it. Why?"

"It's a great old movie. You should catch it sometime." He warmed to his subject as he walked with her to the front of the building. "There's this rich, spoiled kid who falls overboard, and he's rescued by the crew of a fishing vessel. At first he's just like your sister, stuck up, demanding, a real pain in the butt." The warning look on Ginny's face didn't stop him. She couldn't argue with him about her sister's disposition, he thought, at least, not truthfully. "But there's this one fisherman who sees right through him. Sees the good that's buried inside, looking to get free and he sets about making it come out. He puts the kid to work, makes him see what it feels like to pull his own weight, to be part of something. To be proud of what he is for a reason, not because he's a rich man's son. By the end of the movie, he's a regular likable kid."

And he was casting himself as the fisherman, she thought. "What happens to the fisherman?"

"He dies. Gets tangled up in a net and drowns," he said matter-of-factly. "But we don't have to go that far." Quint winked at her.

When he realized that she'd stopped walking next to him, he turned to look at her. "What?"

"Will you stop doing that?"

"Doing what?"

She ran her tongue along her bottom lip, debating not saying anything. And then the words just came out. "Winking at me."

"Why, does it bother you?"

"Yes."

He pulled open the front door and waited until she walked in first. "Good, I'll remember that."

She had the uneasy feeling that he would.

7

"No, that's all right, David, I really don't need rescuing."

Ginny frowned as she conjured up a mental image of the tall, thin man on the other end of the line. He was enjoying this, enjoying her dilemma. She should have known he would.

The moment Quint had gone into the next room, a tiny broom-closetlike area that served as an impromptu kitchen whenever the weather turned too cold to go out for coffee, she had immediately reached for the telephone. Dreading making the call, she'd quickly dialed the number to her law office. She had to let them know that she wasn't coming in for a while.

As soon as she'd gotten David on the line, Quint had walked in. Ginny lowered her voice as much as she could without making it overly obvious that she was whispering.

"Yes, I know I left a pretty strange message on Cliff's machine, but I've managed to iron some of that out." She sighed. "No, I'm not under arrest."

She was sure that David would like nothing better than to tell the senior partners that she was being held in a cell. "But I won't be able to come back to the office for a few days. Ten to be exact." She answered the question fired at her.

She closed her eyes as she listened to the barrage of annoyed words that followed. David Fontaine was her direct superior, a fact he never allowed her to forget for even a moment. Especially when he had tried to hit on her.

"Because I need to be here, that's why." She struggled not to lose her temper. The man was a complete jackass. It wasn't easy letting him into her personal affairs, even a little. "My sister ran afoul of the law here, and she's working off her debt. No, I can't just leave her and come back." She'd known before he said it that David wouldn't understand why she had to remain here with Jenny. The man didn't understand the meaning of the word *family*. "I've left her too much as it is. She's seventeen." She answered his question. "But that doesn't make a difference and lately, neither have I."

Ginny leaned back in the rickety chair, listening to David rake her over the coals about her "lack of loyalty." She passed her hand over her eyes, fighting a headache. Was she blowing up her career? A highly competitive man with no personal life to speak of, Fontaine liked nothing better than knowing that his nearest competition had just gone down a peg, if not several, in the firm's pecking order.

Out of the corner of her eye, she saw Quint watching her. He made no effort to pretend he wasn't listening. At least he was honest, not like some she knew. She would have really rather made this call in private, but privacy, despite this god-forsaken land's lonely terrain, seemed to be at a high premium in Serendipity.

She shifted. Fontaine was winding down. She took the opportunity to jump in.

"If I can get away sooner, I will. I'll let you know," she promised. "I just called so that you can relay the message to Mr. Leary. I know this means the second chair on the case and probably a lot of other cases, too." It took no effort on her part to hear the smug, satisfied note in the voice on the other end. He was practically crowing. She resented what he said next. "No, I'm not letting the team down. I *really* need to be here, David. I'll call you soon." With that, she hung up the phone before he could launch into another round of lectures and re-criminations. "As soon as hell freezes over," she added under her breath.

Reluctantly, she looked up to meet Quint's mildly interested gaze.

"Boyfriend?"

She shivered at the very thought. Good-looking in a prefabricated sort of way, Fontaine had put the moves on her the first week she'd joined the firm. Uninterested, she'd been quick to put him in his place. She didn't doubt that that was in part the reason for the antagonism he displayed toward her.

"Hardly that. He's a junior partner at the law firm where I work. And an all-round royal pain," she added unnecessarily. Rocking back in the chair, she sighed as she dragged her hand through her hair. It rained from her fingers, dark brown waves moodily settling about her shoulders. "Don't worry, I charged the call to my home phone."

"I wasn't worried." Quint had already figured her the type to do the right thing, no matter what. "So you've decided to stay."

Restless, she rose. The small office didn't offer much space for pacing, but she did anyway. "I have no choice, she's my sister."

He leaned back, watching her. She reminded him of a time bomb about to go off. A very attractive, very sensual time bomb. She needed to be defused before it was too late.

"You always have a choice, Geneva. And I'd say that you just made the right one."

She laughed shortly. She could just hear David telling Leary that she'd wantonly disregarded her responsibilities to the firm and gone off on a vacation to some exotic locale in Montana where she couldn't be reached.

God, he could use this to ruin her chances of making partner if he wanted to. Then what would she do? "Tell that to my career."

Quint rose, putting himself in her direct path. He

found it unsettling talking to a moving target. "If you're as good as you say you are, your career shouldn't be put in jeopardy just because you took a few days off to handle a family emergency."

He didn't know what he was talking about, Ginny thought. Safe here in this little hamlet, he had no idea what cutthroat conditions existed in that real world just beyond "his" town's boundaries. There were times, lots of times, when she wished that she didn't know, either. But she did, and that made all the difference in the world. It robbed her of her optimism.

"I am as good as I say I am, but being good isn't enough. Being 110 percent dedicated to the company and 'the team' is what counts."

The team. Man, did she ever hate that term. It had become synonymous with servitude. If it wasn't for the fact that she needed money to pay off the loans she'd taken out to fund her education, she'd be strongly tempted to look for another firm. Maybe just a small office where she could devote herself to making her work count for something instead of worrying about how "the team" felt she was measuring up.

Quint had only heard her side of the conversation, but it was enough. "Seems like they're asking a little too much in my opinion."

Ginny found herself coming to the firm's defense. Now there was a strange set of circumstances. "Nothing more than most firms."

He wasn't arguing that point. "Still doesn't make it right."

"No," she agreed, pressing her lips together. Nothing she could do about this now except ride it out. Quint was right, Jenny needed her to be here, even if Jenny didn't know it. "It doesn't."

Frustrated, Ginny looked around Quint's office. She saw a pile of papers scattered on what looked to be a long wooden table against the far wall. There was a metal four-drawer filing cabinet beside it. A thought vaguely stirred in her head.

"Look, I can't just hang around and do nothing for the next week and a half. Is there anything I can do for you here?"

Quint would have guessed that she'd feel working in the sheriff's office to be beneath her. "Like what?"

She indicated the table. "Do you need your files organized? Provided those are files, of course, and not just mash letters from some frustrated groupie."

The idea of her willingly working for him made him laugh, as did the suggestion about the origin of the papers. "Are you applying for office work?"

Ginny had been an office temp and a waitress among other things to put herself through school. Work was work. "I need to be kept busy."

That wasn't all that she needed in Quint's estimation. "What I think you need is to learn how to let someone else handle the burdens of the world for a change and just learn to take life slow."

Easy for him to say. "If I stop running, I just might lose my balance and fall over."

The wording interested him. He studied her face, curbing the desire to complete the task with his fingertips. "What are you running from?"

Ginny straightened her shoulders like a soldier on the defensive. "Not running from, just running."

"I stand corrected."

But he had a hunch he was right.

It was all working out rather well, Quint mused, glancing over toward Ginny.

Once she'd stopped regarding him as the enemy, Ginny had turned out to be really helpful. She'd bestowed only a few criticisms on the system that was undoubtedly archaic in her estimate. That out of the way, she plowed through the clutter and filed the forms he'd forced himself to fill out but never put away over the course of the past two years. He appreciated the help. Appreciated, too, the enhancement that was being made to his office by her very presence.

She was a hell of a lot easier on the eye than Carly was.

Ginny moved by him to put away the final handful of forms. He caught a whiff of that same stirring scent he'd been aware of the past few hours. It seemed to fill every small space around him. He put down his pen, surrendering to it.

"What is that?"

She closed the metal drawer and looked at him quizzically. "What?"

"That perfume you're wearing."

For a second, she had to stop and think. "I'm not wearing any perfume." She couldn't smell anything but he obviously could. "Must be my shampoo."

Wasn't like any shampoo he was acquainted with. "You smell like a field of wildflowers in the summer."

Was it her imagination, or was he being poetic? Ginny tried not to let the comment affect her. "Is that good?"

She could almost feel his eyes as they washed over her body, yet there wasn't anything invasive about it. "I think so."

It was happening again, that strange, nervous little tic moving through her in response to the way he looked at her.

Determined to shake free of it, she pushed the drawer closed and cleared her throat.

"Well, I'm finished." Ginny glanced at the now-empty table. "Who would have ever thought such a little town could have generated so much paperwork?"

Quint thought of all the things he was called upon to do. Granted, there were no random shootings to plague him, but there were a host of other things. Enough to keep a grown man busy every day of his life. Most required some sort of notations made.

Quint laughed. "You'd be surprised."

She'd filed for some time and read some of the reports out of curiosity before putting them away. Ginny shook her head. "Not anymore."

She was going to start being restless again, he could sense it. Quint rose from his desk. Time to make the rounds. Carly still hadn't come back from Taylor's, but Quint had a pretty good hunch he knew why. There was more than a little interest in his cousin's blue eyes when he looked at Jenny.

"Want to see how Jenny's getting along?" Quint suggested.

She was sorely tempted, but she knew how Jenny would take that. "Yes, but I didn't want her to think I'm spying on her."

She was right. That might set things back. Quint reached for his hat. "Tell you what, I'll go check on her for you, then report back."

He was being awfully nice. She was beginning to feel guilty about having given him such a hard time yesterday. "You really don't have to do that."

He was already at the door. "I'm a public servant," he reminded her. "And you're the public."

She crossed to him. "But I'm not part of your public."

Gliding a finger down her nose, he smiled into her face. "For now you are."

Funny how a simple look could manage to ignite her. "Thank you."

"No problem." He closed the door behind him, leaving her alone.

But there was, she thought. And there would be until she straightened Jenny out.

"So, how was your first day?"

Alerted by the sound of the front door opening, Zoe came out of the kitchen to greet them. Warm, tempting smells followed in her wake. Quint's mother looked at Jenny, waiting for an answer.

Jenny lifted one shoulder, then let it drop in a careless response. "It was okay."

"Mr. Taylor says that you're a good worker once you put your mind to it," Quint told her as he removed his holster and set it on the side table.

Jenny tried to appear indifferent to the unsolicited compliment. She'd expected no comment from the old man, or, if he did comment, that it would be criticism. To hear that he'd praised her robbed Jenny of her edge and her weapon. There was nothing to flare against, no emotion to hide behind.

Without anything to hide behind, she felt vulnerable and lost.

She turned to look at Quint. "He did?"

"Yes." He knew that would get to her. "He said it's too bad you don't live around here because then he'd offer you the job."

Ginny reacted instantly. That's all she needed, to have Jenny think about dropping out and getting a job. Her sister disliked high school as it was. "She's still in school."

Quint never missed a beat as he smoothed over the bumpy terrain. "Part-time once school started, of course."

Ginny saw the tinge of pride in her sister's face. Her own heart swelled at the sight of it and at the thought that Jenny was finally doing something productive with herself, however temporary.

She slanted a look toward Quint. He'd been right after all. Maybe a scene or two out of *Captains Courageous* was what Jenny had needed all along.

"Got an answer for everything, don't you?" she asked, amused.

"Not everything," he allowed, crossing to her. "But so far, you're asking the right questions."

Zoe watched the exchange between the two. A warm feeling about them began to take shape. She was very intuitive when it came to her sons. She'd known Kent and Will were falling in love even before they did. And now look, her boys were all getting married within a few weeks of each other. This was already shaping up to be a fall to remember. And Quint definitely had the signs that this young woman might be the one to finally send him off to buy a double bed for his house.

"Hank called," she told him nonchalantly. "Said

he'd try to be here by the weekend to go over what he wants for the wedding."

Quint smiled. "Fiona should be enough."

Yes, Zoe thought, Quint definitely had the signs.

Ginny looked at him, curious. Her own family had been completely devoid of any interaction. She hadn't even known her mother had family until they'd come to the funeral. Without fully realizing she was doing it, she was gravitating toward his, hungry for details.

"Fiona?"

"Hank's fiancée," Quint told her. He stole an apple from the fruit bowl on the coffee table and took a bite. "They met when he accidentally faxed his résumé to her number."

"And a lucky thing that mistake was, too," Zoe told them with feeling. "I was beginning to think he'd never get married. A different girl every weekend when he was in high school and college. He was the charmer in the family."

Ginny glanced over toward the fireplace. There were clusters of framed photographs all across the wide mantel, depicting the Cutler siblings at various stages of their lives. To varying degrees, all the brothers looked alike. All were blond with deep blue eyes, strong chins and heart-melting smiles. If asked, she would have said that the whole lot looked like charmers.

"Hey," Quint protested, "I thought I was." He

caught his mother about the waist from behind, giving her a bear hug that reeked of affection.

Zoe slapped him away. "You were the silver-tongued devil of the lot." She glanced at Ginny. "Still are, no doubt."

He pretended that the remark appeased him. "Same thing."

She eyed her son, shaking her head. "Not exactly." Zoe turned toward Ginny, inspired. Sons still needed their mothers to move things along. "Geneva, would you do me a favor?"

"Anything." The unqualified promise, even though it came from her own lips, caught Ginny by surprise again. She was never that free and easy with her words, not even with Jenny. Maybe there was something about this little town that changed people, she mused.

"Get him out of my hair." To emphasize her point, Zoe pushed Quint toward Ginny. As an afterthought, she took the half-eaten apple from his hand. "Take him out on the porch until dinner is on the table."

Quint spread his hands wide as he stood before Ginny. "You heard the lady. Take me somewhere."

Ginny could feel her own mouth widening in a grin to match his. This lighthearted feeling was infectious. "You don't strike me as someone who could be led around by the nose."

"Not by the nose," he agreed, "but by the hand

might not be a bad notion.'' He held it out to her.
When she didn't take it, he took hers instead and
began drawing her toward the front door.

She didn't go unwillingly.

Ginny paused only long enough to look over her
shoulder at Zoe. The older woman had taken charge
of Jenny and was taking her into the kitchen. Jenny
looked almost happy to go.

Don't look now, Ginny thought, *but we've stum-
bled into a full-fledged miracle.*

Quint saw where she was looking. ''She's
okay,'' he assured Ginny softly.

Ginny raised her eyes to his and realized that
maybe she was standing just a tad too close for her
own safety. She couldn't quite get herself to put the
right amount of space between them. Or any, for
that matter.

''Yes, I know she is. I just can't stop being concerned about her, that's all.''

Quint eased the door closed behind him. He liked
her out here like this, with the moon filtering star-
dust down around her and a feeling that there was
just the two of them in the world. Made a man think
about the things that were still missing in his life.
He considered himself blessed and his life full, except in one respect. He'd also always felt that when
the time was right, he'd know.

He thought he knew now.

''Well, you shouldn't,'' he said to her. She
looked up at him, slightly puzzled. ''Stop, I mean.

You shouldn't stop caring about her or being concerned, that's only natural. But you don't have to let it consume you, either. Jenny'll be all right." That shampoo of hers was driving him crazy, he thought. Got right in under a man's skin and made him think about things that he'd like to do with a woman. A very special woman. "Took a bit of doing, she managed to fit right in today. Taylor was very satisfied with her."

His voice had lowered and was enveloping her now like the warm evening breeze. Ginny could have sworn that every hair on her body was standing on end. Waiting. She had to swallow before she answered.

"That was your doing."

"I wasn't there," he reminded her, his breath rippling along her face.

She drew in a shaky breath, telling herself she was behaving like a silly schoolgirl, for heaven's sake. If he knew what was on her mind, he'd laugh at her.

"No, I mean that you made her work off her debt. You had her come to work for Mr. Taylor and that seems to be making a difference." It took effort to force out every word when all she could do was look at his mouth, his firm, sensual mouth and ache to have him kiss her again.

Boy, this was a change. She was never like this.

"We do what we can."

"Yes," she said, sighing, "we do."

He'd held out as long as a man possibly could, he thought. "Geneva?"

If he didn't kiss her soon, she was afraid that she was going to make a fool of herself and kiss him. "Hmm?"

"Would you mind very much if I kissed you again?"

Finally! She could feel her heart slam against her rib cage like a basketball being slam-dunked. Her lips felt dry as she said, "On one condition."

Quint crooked his index finger beneath the point of her chin and tilted it back until their eyes met. "And that being—?"

Her tongue slid along her paper-dry lips. "That you stop calling me Geneva. I've always hated the name. It's old-fashioned and awful."

"No, it's not," he said softly, his words skimming along her skin. "There's nothing awful about you." His arms closed around her.

There was no place for this in her life, Ginny thought. Absolutely no place, no room. Her life was filled to the brim with responsibilities. This had no future, practically no present.

But all the logic in the world didn't seem to work. She was completely focused on his mouth, on the anticipation of feeling it against her own.

Maybe this was a mistake, she thought, but it was a mistake she was willing to make. At least for now. "Your mother was right."

His mouth curved in amusement. "Oh?"

"You are a silver-tongued devil."

That didn't seem to bother her, he noticed. "Mothers generally know what they're talking about when it comes to their kids."

His words struck a nerve, but she refused to let it get to her. "Mine didn't."

He'd forgotten about that. Looking into her eyes tended to make him forget a great many things. "I don't feel like arguing tonight, Counselor."

Without being fully aware of what she was doing, she snuggled against him. It amazed her how well her body fit against his. As if they were meant to stand like this, bodies touching, adrenaline pumping. "What do you feel like doing?"

Quint laughed, framing her face with his hands. "Guess."

She didn't have to, because the next moment, he showed her.

8

The sensation coursing through her body was hot, demanding and all-consuming.

It made her afraid, really afraid.

She was afraid to feel this exhilarated, this completely, blindingly overwhelmed.

For one shining minute, there was nothing else, no earth, no sky, no world. No beings except for Quint, except for her. And no other thoughts except those that centered on this man and what he was doing to her simply by kissing her.

There was nothing "simply" about it.

It was the most overpowering sensation Ginny had ever encountered, even more overpowering than her own iron determination to dig herself and her sister out of the poverty-laced, dead-end world they had been born to. That had galvanized her, strengthened her in a world that was out to undermine her.

This, this was completely different.

This weakened her, took her breath away, dissolved her mind and had her clinging to his arms like some fragile blossom tossed about in a gale.

She had no control over it, no control at all. And that frightened her more than anything.

She was the one, Quint realized, his body quickening. The one who knocked his hat off his head, who slid his boots off his feet. She was the one who could and would make him jump through any hoop she held up for him.

He had enjoyed, completely and without reservation, the opposite sex ever since Janet Walsh had kissed him during recess. He'd been thirteen at the time and had been hooked on ladies ever since.

But there had never been this feeling of coming together, of something more than pleasure happening beneath the surface. There was a stirring in his system that was generated by something more than friendship and attraction. There was something extra here, something he couldn't name or quite understand beyond the fact that this lady lawyer with her whip-sharp temper and her flashing eyes was the one.

He'd bet his life on it.

Quint drew his head back, wanting just to look at her face, to see if there was a sign that indicated she even remotely felt the same thing he was experiencing so vividly.

One look into her dazed eyes when Ginny opened them again told Quint all he wanted to know.

Very slowly, feeling his way around this newly discovered terrain, he ran his hands up her arms. His eyes on hers, he brushed his thumbs along the sides of her neck. He saw the pulse in her throat jump in response, heard the small, almost imperceptible intake of breath as she tried to appear unaffected.

Yup, he wasn't wrong about her. They belonged together.

It was a little startling for a thirty-one-year-old man to look his destiny in the face like this, but he'd always prided himself on adjusting quickly to any situation. He adjusted now.

The very next moment, the face of his destiny clouded over.

Ginny pushed him back. Force and bravado were her only line of defense. She had nothing else to grasp. "You've got to stop doing that."

Cocking his head, Quint studied her, trying to understand why she felt it necessary to hold him at arm's length after the fact. There was no need for pretenses between them. He hadn't been alone in that kiss.

"Why? If I don't miss my guess, you like it as much as I do."

"I don't, I mean I d—" Indignant, it took her a moment longer to process his words than it should have. "You like it?"

"Darlin'—" grin curving his mouth, he slid his

hands along her arms again "—if you can't tell that then I'm definitely doing something wrong."

"Hey, save the dessert for later, you two. Ma said to tell you dinner's on the table and to get yourselves in now."

She hadn't realized that they had an audience. A flush raced up her neck and cheeks marking its path in heat as she swung around. The next moment she was looking up at a man who looked like a slightly thinner, ever so slightly younger version of the man who had just now rendered her entire world a disaster area by the power in his lips.

Draping his arm easily over her shoulders, Quint figured that introductions were in order. "Geneva Marlow, this uncouth oaf is my brother Kent, the one who thinks he runs the Shady Lady for my folks."

Kent inclined his head, his blue eyes unabashedly taking measure of her. They had the same smile, Ginny thought. How was it that one smile left her feeling practically disembodied and the other had no effect on her at all?

"Pleased to meet you, Geneva." He took her hand and shook it. Ginny felt the calluses that came from hard manual work. "And for the record," he confided, "I have plenty of couth. Quint just doesn't know how to recognize it, that's all." Dropping her hand, he held open the door for her. "But he certainly knows how to recognize a lovely lady."

Quint hooted. When Kent raised a questioning brow, Quint explained his amusement. "Well, Brianne did the impossible, I see."

Kent shook his head, obviously missing something. "How's that?"

Quint followed Ginny in, keeping a proprietary hand on her shoulder, just in case there was any question in his brother's mind just what the situation was here. "She turned a sow's ear into a silk purse."

Happier these days because of his approaching marriage than he could ever recall being, Kent pretended to take offense. "Who're you calling a sow's ear?"

Peering out of the high-ceilinged dining room, Zoe called to her sons. "Mind your manners, you two. Remember, we have guests."

Zoe smiled to herself as her sons filed by her. It had been a long time since she'd uttered words to that effect in earnest. Then, like as not flying fists would have accompanied the raised voices. Now the words were said in jest.

She saw them far too infrequently to please her mother's heart. It was a real treat whenever any of her brood turned up at the table. Two just made it that much more so.

And soon, she knew, there were going to be a lot more faces at her table, turning up with regular frequency. With three weddings in the offing and all three couples setting up housekeeping in the area, her house was destined to ring of familiar voices forever on.

Just the way she'd always dreamed it would be when she had first exchanged vows with Jake.

She looked at her husband now as they all sat down at the long table he'd made her for their very first wedding anniversary. No chairs, just a long table and the promise to fill it with chairs and children to sit in them. The table was her most prized possession.

Zoe's eyes swept thoughtfully over Jake. He'd been unusually quiet today, ever since noon when he'd returned from town. She knew him inside out. Something was wrong, and he wasn't telling her.

She'd give him a little longer.

Turning toward Quint, she said, "Ceely Watts's mother said Ceely was going to have a big party this weekend to celebrate her twenty-first birthday. She asked to borrow our wagon because they want to have an old-fashioned hayride for the kids." She disregarded Kent's audible groan. "We're all invited." Zoe slanted a look at Ginny. "I thought that perhaps you might take Jenny and Geneva to the party, Quint."

Leaning over to help himself to some of the fresh-baked loaf on the side of the table, Kent laughed as he shook his head doubtfully. "I don't know if the sheriff of Serendipity's up to handling two lovely ladies."

Her attention momentarily drawn away from

both her husband and the proposed party, Zoe took another, longer look at Kent. Of all of them, he was the one who had frequented their table most, the one who had opted to make ranching his life rather than trying to get as far away from it as possible.

Lovely ladies, was it? "What's gotten into you, Kent?" Zoe asked.

The remark was one she would have never expected from her middle son. It was more in keeping with something that Jake might say. Instead, he sat quietly at his place, hardly touching the food on his plate.

Quint smiled, helping himself to a serving of sliced pork. "He's in love, Ma. Makes all the difference in the world, doesn't it, Kent?"

Quint prided himself on helping his brother over the last hump. Knocking some sense into his head to get him to go to New York and finally propose to Brianne Gainsborough before Kent allowed the best thing that ever happened to him to fade out of his life after her photograph assignment was over.

The old Kent would have bristled at the observation, said a few choice words and left the table. Or merely stormed off in silence. Instead, rather than become annoyed that his private affairs had been aired before strangers, Kent could only nod.

"Yeah, it does."

Zoe couldn't stand it any longer. She'd given her husband enough time to either share his problem with her or come to terms with it. But instead, he'd just sat there, looking as if he'd lost his best friend in the world. Enough was enough. With a clatter, Zoe retired her silverware.

"All right, old man, what's going on? What's the matter with you?"

Jake looked up, his mind a long way from the conversation at the table, a conversation which normally would have warmed his heart. The life refused to return to his eyes. He sighed without realizing that he did so. "Nothing."

Zoe saw her sons exchange uneasy glances. "Nothing, my foot. You've been acting like someone I don't know all afternoon." Concern softened her voice. Having lived through seeing her husband have one heart attack, she existed under the constant specter of his having another despite all her pains to keep him healthy. "You're not feeling sick again, are you?"

Disgusted with himself, with everything, Jake gained his feet, throwing his napkin down. "No. Can't a man have a little peace and quiet when he wants it?" He turned from the table.

"Not in this family." Determined, Zoe followed him out. "Now, what is it?" Her voice was low, coaxing, masking frustrated exasperation. "I'm your life's partner, Jake, you're not supposed to have any problems without sharing them with me."

Emotionally cornered, aware that he was the focal point of everyone's attention, he sighed, scrubbing his hands over his face. "We might lose the ranch."

The barely whispered statement had Quint and Kent on their feet in an instant. In the next, they were at their father's side, disbelief and shock mingling in their faces.

The fact that this was none of her business didn't shackle Ginny's movements. She was directly behind them.

Agitation feathered all through Kent's system, but he managed to keep it under control.

"Why?" Kent demanded.

The story was so confused, it swam like cloudy chicken soup through his mind. Jake plucked at the chunks of information, but even talking about it was painful.

"It seems that when this property was originally purchased from the Macabees, the right papers weren't signed, or notarized, or—" He dragged an impatient hand through his full head of hair. "Hell, I don't understand it, but now Jeb Macabee's son is serving notice that the property legally still belongs to them, and we've got thirty days to pay up or leave. There's no way we can pay the true value of this property in today's terms."

His distress was tangible, Ginny thought. He looked like a man who'd failed his family somehow.

"We need a lawyer," Kent interjected.

"There's Eli Jackson over in Carnes," Zoe reminded him. "He did our wills right after you came home from the hospital."

"You'll have to go see him first thing tomorrow," Kent agreed. But Quint was looking at Ginny.

Ginny knew what he was asking. She placed a hand on Jake's arm. "Where do you have your papers?"

Zoe turned to look at her, as if forgetting in the heat of the moment that she was, after all, a lawyer and might be able to help.

His mind unfocused, misery in his eyes, it took Jake a second to realize that the question was coming from Ginny. "What?"

"Your papers," she repeated. She saw quiet pleasure entering Quint's eyes but forced herself to focus on Jake. "Everything you have pertaining to the purchase and running of this property, do you still have them?" She imagined that it would be a simple enough matter to straighten out for someone who knew what they were doing. Legal terms tended to intimidate a lot of people.

Jake shook his head. "There was a fire, took half the house."

"And the papers?" She knew what was coming before he answered.

"Were in that part of the house," Zoe concluded.

"I always meant to get them replaced, but one thing after another kept getting in the way...."

Jake's voice trailed off. And now it looked as if it was too late.

Not about to be put off by inconvenience, Ginny took another approach. "All right. Deeds have to be recorded, titles transferred. Records have to be kept somewhere." She turned toward Quint. Serendipity looked too small to have its own bureau of records, although she might be mistaken. "Where would the nearest bureau of records be?"

"It's in Billings," Quint told her. "I can run you up there tomorrow."

"Good, run me," she agreed. She looked at the older couple. "Do you have anything at all I can look at in the meantime? Anything," she emphasized. "Any shred, any scrap you have pertaining to the ranch, I don't care how small. I want to see everything."

Jake was beginning to feel better. The girl looked like a scrapper. He liked her style a lot better than Eli's.

"That's a mountain of paper," he warned, thinking of the mortgage receipts, the tax forms and insurance stubs he'd retained. He had no idea if that was what she meant, but it was something.

She dismissed his concern. "I've scaled mountains before."

The thing Ginny hated most in the world were people who took advantage of other people. Her thoughts returned to Dewey as she glanced toward Jenny. The sheriff from Smoke Tree had tried to take advantage of the dire circumstances she'd found herself in. There'd been no way to make him pay for what he'd attempted to trade on. He'd wanted her to sleep with him in exchange for certain comforts and favors. Things had threatened to get very ugly. She'd counted herself lucky that she and Jenny had managed to get away before anything had happened to them. But at the very least, she could try to help here.

"All right." The cloud that had hung over him ever since Jake had spoken to Macabee's lawyer began to break up. "When do you want them?"

"Now."

"It can wait until after dinner," Zoe informed her. "You'll work better on a full stomach."

"I work better," Ginny corrected her, "on adrenaline." And Zoe's son, she added silently, had already supplied that—in spades.

Ginny turned on her heel, following Jake out of the room. She missed the look of admiration on Quint's face.

"Make up a tray, Ma," he told her. "I'll bring it in to her in a little while."

Zoe nodded, her eyes nervously following Jake and Ginny as they left.

"So, how's it going?"

Quint poked his head into his parents' small den that Ginny had completely commandeered. She'd been at this over two days.

You would have thought, he mused, that she was putting together evidence to plead before the Supreme Court. Taking her to Billings, he'd been forced to leave her for the day. When he'd returned to pick her up, he'd found that she'd traced the ranch's title not just back to Macabee, but to the family of the man who had sold it to him. She'd stood at the curb before the closed bureau of records office, waiting for him, a stack of papers under her arm and a very satisfied look on her face.

A look that he'd wanted to share—and did by impulsively kissing her the moment he had her alone. There was no question about it, the lady stirred his blood.

She looked worn now as she looked up at him. Worn but very satisfied with herself. This was what she did best, he thought. She loved it and it showed. Lucky for his parents.

Ginny leaned back in the chair. The old leather chair creaked and groaned at every movement. A little like her shoulders, she thought, rotating her neck. The aches and stiffness refused to retreat. She'd been hunched over the desk for what seemed like an eternity now, taking breaks only to make calls and join her sister and the others for a meal. Just long enough to notice that Jenny seemed a great deal more animated than she usually did.

But it was all worth it.

She let out a long breath, unaware that she was being dramatic. "It's going," she answered.

Quint picked up the yellow legal pad she'd been writing on, glancing at it to get a clue. Page after page was filled with small, strange scratchings. The woman had handwriting like the tail of a cat dipped in ink. He could only make out about half, and not well at that.

He let the pad drop back on the desk. "Is that cautious lawyer talk?"

She laughed. It did sound like that, didn't it? She hadn't meant it to.

"You found me out. Actually, I think that Mr. Macabee's lawyer is trying to pull a sleight of hand on your father." She saw storm clouds gathering in his eyes. He was easygoing, except when it came to people he loved, she thought. She liked that. "These kinds of things aren't unheard of." As sheriff, he had to be aware of that. "Hustlers come in all sizes and shapes and wander through all walks of life." Passing a hand over her eyes, she wished a headache away. It lingered anyway. "Any reason he picked now rather than some other time?"

Yeah, there was a reason, Quint thought. A good one. Macabee was slime. "The Shady Lady is doing really well, thanks to Kent's management and the town's growth spurt. We're even getting an amusement park, thanks in part to Denise, Will's fiancée," he interjected to keep her from getting confused. "She sold the town her carnival rides. Because of its location, the ranch has become prime real estate."

He knew that because, after his father's attack, he'd looked into selling the property to pay the bills. It would have not only paid off the debts, but set his parents up nicely. But no one in the family wanted to see the ranch go, so the five of them had pooled what money they could to pay off the bills. Kent had taken over running it to give his father time to properly recover. After his father was well, by mutual agreement, Kent just continued doing what he was doing.

"Well, it's real estate that's going to stay in your family," she promised. "I'm meeting with Macabee's lawyer tomorrow to set things straight." She was looking forward to it. If the man wanted a fight, so much the better. She could use a good fight to sink her teeth into and help clear the cobwebs from her mind.

He wanted it straight. "Is there a chance that we could still lose the ranch?"

She drew together the piles of papers she'd been examining and neatened them beneath her pad. "Only if Macabee and his lawyer try to take it from your parents at gunpoint."

That was reassuring. Hooking his thumbs in his belt, his palm rested against his holster. "I don't think that'll be a problem."

Her eyes shifted to the hilt of his handgun. "Ever used that thing?"

He knew what she was asking. "Against a man, no, but I've wounded many a tin can."

She laughed, then winced as the sound rippled through her. She was stiffer than she thought.

"What is it?"

"Nothing." She waved away the note of concern she heard in his voice, warmed by it even as she felt foolish for reacting like that. "It's just sitting in a chair all these hours has made me a little stiff. I'm not up to any sudden movements," she explained.

Quint pretended to assess her. "You don't look stiff. As a matter of fact, you look rather supple. Warm and supple."

She wasn't supposed to be taken in by charm. So why was she? "I didn't think that small-town sheriffs were so smooth."

He circled behind her. "You have a lot to learn about small towns."

"Apparently." Ginny assumed he was leaving her to her work. When she felt his hands on her shoulders, she jerked slightly before recovering, biting off a few choice words in the interim.

Quint laughed. The lady could probably turn the air blue if she wanted to, he guessed, amused by the thought. "Shh, just sit still and I'll see what I can do about working those kinks out of your back."

Every touch, every movement, had repercussions that echoed through her. He might be working the kinks out, but he was definitely working something else in. This was definitely not helping her think. Ginny tried to shift away.

"I don't think that's such a good idea."

Quint continued as if she hadn't said anything. "Why?"

She tried to shift again, but his hands gently restrained her, keeping her where she was. Between heaven and hell. Tingling sensations were beginning to form and take hold, dissolving her where she sat. "Because I can't think when you do that."

"Then it's a very good idea." He turned the chair around until she faced him. Taking her hand, he eased her up to her feet. "I think you've been thinking too much today."

Her throat felt dry. And her palms felt damp. "Is that your professional opinion?"

"Absolutely."

She'd missed dinner, Quint noticed. His mother had brought in a tray, but it stood beside the papers, barely touched. He supposed she was consumed by her work. That was both good and bad. Nice to be that dedicated, but not to the exclusion of everything else. Because the effort was to help his parents, he didn't comment on it. But he wanted to make sure the lady didn't slip back to her old ways. She had to see that work and life could coexist.

"Why don't you come out and see if the moon's still in the same place it was yesterday."

Amusement played along the corners of her mouth. "You mean it travels?"

He laced his fingers through hers, coaxing her out of the stuffy den. "Out here, you never know."

Ginny struggled not to sigh as their palms touched.

9

Quint eased the door closed behind him before turning toward Ginny. He wanted to be absolutely sure she wasn't hiding anything from him. "So my parents really have nothing to worry about?"

"No."

And being able to say that gave Ginny a great deal more pleasure than she'd experienced of late winning in court. This felt so much more real, so much more satisfying than undertaking battles for behemoth corporations that had no face, no heart. This mattered. This, she realized with a pang, was what she was meant to do. But not right now. Right now, she had another life waiting for her.

Maybe someday.

"I think Macabee is hoping to capitalize on the fact that your father lost the papers that were signed in the fire. From what I gather, it wasn't a secret." Digging through records and possible tie-ins at the local newspaper office, she'd found that the fire had been the talk of the town the week it happened. "I found everything I needed at the records office."

There was no need to mention that the search, since it was paper that she'd been looking for and not data recorded on the computer, had taken her the better part of a day. That was all behind her, all just part of the battle. A battle that she already considered won.

"There's still some minor confusion to be cleared up—" such as how Macabee's lawyer thought he could ethically get away with this, she thought "—but when you unwrap all the legal mumbo jumbo, the title to the Shady Lady was legally transferred from Macabee to your father, and we have proof." She grinned, feeling like the heroic Mountie, saving the beleaguered heroine from the evil clutches of the greedy villain in an old-fashioned melodrama. "The old homestead is safe."

Quint wondered if she knew that her eyes were sparkling as she spoke. This had mattered to her almost as much as it had to them. He found that very interesting. And heartening.

He slipped his arm around her. "They'll be very happy to hear that. We all are." His eyes held hers and said things to her he couldn't put into words. Yet. "I can't thank you enough."

She was having trouble concentrating again. It happened every time he was so close to her. Close enough to tempt, close enough to kiss. She found her tongue and focused on making words come out of her mouth instead of a sigh.

"It's not anything any good lawyer wouldn't have been able to do, given time."

Always alert, he widened the opening she had unknowingly created for him.

"That's just it, Serendipity doesn't have a good lawyer, or any lawyer for that matter. If anyone needs a lawyer here, they have to go clear to the next town to get one. Or farther if they want a good one," he added, thinking of the attorney Macabee had retained. Even the one his parents occasionally used was only good for the most minor of undertakings.

In Southern California, for the most part, one town or city fed directly into another, Ginny realized. Here, going to the next town meant a considerable trip. She could see the difficulty.

She shrugged and was immediately aware that her shoulders were brushing against his arm. More warmth spread. "I know people who would say a lawyer-free town's a good thing."

He smiled down into her face. "That's because they never met you."

Her stomach tightened. "Is that a compliment, or are you just flushed from knowing that the Shady Lady stays in the family?"

"Both, but you don't need anything extra in your arsenal for a man to take notice of you or give you a compliment. You stir a man's blood just by standing there."

The feeling, she wanted to say, was more than

mutual. But then that would be giving him insight into what was going on in her head and she didn't want that. That would give him an advantage over her. She'd learned long ago to play her hand close to her chest and trust no one.

She wanted to trust him. Wanted to be with him. Wanted.

But even as the desire rose, Ginny knew it couldn't have an outlet. She couldn't start something that would have to be finished in a very short space of time. As soon as Jenny paid her "debt" to Serendipity society, they'd be on their way—no looking back. She had a life waiting for her back in California. A high-speed life where she had to struggle to catch her breath, but it was a life she'd forged for herself. A life that until recently she thought she desperately wanted.

Now she wasn't all that sure.

Ginny didn't know what she wanted. No, that wasn't strictly true. She didn't know what she could allow herself to want.

When he drew her into his arms, she felt wariness forming within her again. Not because she didn't trust him or what he would do—that was gone—but because she didn't trust what she was feeling when he touched her, didn't trust herself to act rationally.

His mouth was a fraction away from hers when she wedged her hands up against his chest. "Is Jenny with your mother?"

Surprised, Quint stopped. He wasn't about to force himself on her. His hands loosened about her waist. "No, Jenny's still in Serendipity."

It was after six. The general store, she knew, closed at five. "Working?" Had Taylor kept her after hours to do inventory?

"No, as a matter of fact, Taylor let her off early today so that Carly could take her to Sadie's." She was skittish. He could see it in her eyes. Raised around horses all his life, he knew animal fear when he saw it. What he didn't understand was why. He hadn't really done anything that he hadn't before. He hadn't even kissed her.

Ginny tried to remember if he'd mentioned the person before and couldn't. "And that would be—?"

Built over twenty years ago, the small establishment was still considered new. "The local place where all the kids her age hang out. It's where my brothers, Morgan and I hung out when we were younger." He supposed, by her standards, it was antiquated, but there was something to be said for that. Knowing their kids were there set parents' minds at ease.

Jenny wouldn't have gone there on her own. Ginny scrutinized Quint's face, trying hard not to notice that looking at him sent quivers of anticipation through her. "Is that part of your rehabilitation program for Jenny?"

He laughed. "Smart lady."

His words struck her as ironic. "If I was so smart, there'd be no need to 'rehabilitate' Jenny. She would have turned out right to begin with." She still wasn't sure where she'd taken the wrong path or when, but she obviously had because Jenny was so troubled.

"Don't be so hard on yourself." His voice was soft, comforting. Something within her longed to lose herself in him, even though she knew it was wrong. "No one can do everything, and you had your hands full just providing for her."

That was no excuse and she didn't accept it. "Your mother raised five of you."

Her view of the situation was far too narrow, Quint thought. Maybe that was the problem. She concentrated on one thing to the exclusion of all else. In his estimation, she needed to do less, and that way, accomplish more all around.

"My mother," he pointed out, "had my father, and we all did our part at different times, pitching in. From what you've told me, I'm gathering that you had only you to fall back on."

That was true enough. As far back as she could remember, there'd never been anyone else to turn to. No one to talk to or trust. Or surrender the burden to, even for a little while. Her mother had been far too busy partying to be a mother. There'd been only her. And she had messed up royally. "Emphasis on the word *fall*."

He wasn't about to stand by and let her do this

to herself. For once, someone had to take her side, even if she didn't.

"Now, this is my town," he said gently, "and I told you not to be hard on yourself. Haven't you learned that you should listen to the sheriff?"

Ginny reacted to the kindness she heard, to the teasing. It felt good. "Or what—you'll throw me into jail again?"

He nodded, pulling his lips into a stern line. "This time there'll be hard time involved."

From nowhere, excitement rippled through her. She realized it had to do with the look in his eyes. He looked at her as if she were a woman, a desirable woman. He made her want to live up to the image.

"You almost make me want to break the law."

When he gathered her into his arms this time, it felt as natural as if it had been happening since the beginning of time. "You really are something else, Ginny Marlow." And then the laughter on his lips softened as he looked at her, debating. He risked the question. "Would you consider staying here? After Jenny settles her debt, I mean."

Was he asking her to stay? Or was it just an interested question?

In either case, she couldn't. The triumph she felt in helping the Marlows with their legal problem notwithstanding, it wasn't possible for her to give up her life in California. And her future.

But something within her yearned anyway.

"Not right away, but maybe someday. This seems a peaceful enough town to come back to." And then she laughed, surprised to hear herself say that. "I never thought I'd even ever consider living in a place that doesn't have at least a ten-story building in its midst."

Quint arched one light brown brow. "Height important to you?"

He probably thought she was insane. "Only insomuch as it reflects civilization."

She needed to see things in the right light and not let her past color it. "That's all around you, Ginny. It all depends on the type of civilization you're looking for."

He didn't understand, Ginny thought. Didn't know what it had taken for her to get where she was. Didn't know how afraid she was of sliding back.

"I'm looking for somewhere where the odds are on my side, where I can make a good living for myself and my sister." She let him a little further into her life. "Where I can have everything I didn't have when I was growing up."

She was confusing possessions with security. He could see that happening. "Seems to me that a great deal of that would be taken care of if you just had love to start with."

Love was something she'd never had, even though she'd ached for it as a child. But she'd made her peace with that, the way an adult did with the height they'd reached. It was just the way things were, no use wishing for anything else, anything more. She wouldn't know what to do with love now if it came her way. She saw it as a weakness, not an asset. Love made you put your guard down. And then all hell could break loose.

"Maybe," she allowed, "but I've learned never to trust anything or anyone but myself."

He felt for her. A great deal. "Pretty lonely that way."

She shrugged carelessly, moving away. "But safe."

Quint didn't see it that way. "Safe isn't always good. Safe can be very stifling."

"That's a strange sentiment for a sheriff to have. Why did you become a sheriff, anyway? I have a feeling you could have been anything you wanted to be."

"I am what I wanted to be. In Serendipity, I'm the police chief, I'm the head detective and a little more than half the police force." He smiled. "Growing up, I was always the peacemaker every time my brothers and sister got into it. Came natural. I like restoring the peace. Makes me feel as if I'm accomplishing something." He could see that she was restless. Maybe she'd feel better with the others.

He nodded toward the sky. "Now that we've established that the moon is in place, among a few other things, why don't we go back inside?"

Ginny felt his hand at the small of her back. The less time she spent alone with Quint, the better. She wasn't all that confident that she could keep herself in check.

"All right."

She wouldn't have believed it if she hadn't seen it with her own eyes.

Ginny was seeing it with her own eyes and she *still* didn't know whether or not to believe it. In the past week, the change in Jenny had been nothing short of overwhelming.

Oh, she still wasn't the warm, sunny girl that Ginny remembered and carried around in her heart, the little girl who had looked to her for everything. But the belligerence, the thumbing-her-nose-at-the-world attitude was gone, thank God. And there was a glow about Jenny, a zest rather than the I-don't-give-a-damn behavior that had been the hallmark of everything that Jenny had done in the past couple of years. It had gotten to the point that it pervaded the very air between them.

Most incredible of all was that Jenny talked, actually talked to her. Not just at the table when two or more of the Cutlers were present to hear, but in the bedroom that they were sharing for the duration of their stay.

This was *just* like the old days, Ginny thought as she got ready for bed later that night. The old days when they were still children and she would fall asleep to the sound of her sister's voice, or vice versa. They would lie awake at night and talk for hours of what was to be and what happiness their future would hold. Anything to keep the world that held them prisoner back then at bay.

In a strange way, Ginny mused, those little snippets of time were the happiest she could recall. Until recently.

Tonight Jenny's conversation was littered with the names of the people she'd met at the drive-through that Carly had taken her to. Sadie's was the closest thing Serendipity had to a fast-food restaurant and the only place, aside from the cinema duplex, where teens felt as if they could be themselves for a while.

Jenny talked of nothing else but Sadie's since Carly had dropped her off. Ginny noticed that more than a few sentences were devoted to someone named Billy.

Jenny wiggled out of her jeans, leaving them where they were on the floor. "They said he'd be at the hayride."

Programmed for neatness, Ginny automatically reached for the jeans and folded them over the back of the chair. "Hayride?"

Jenny looked at her impatiently. "The one on Saturday, you remember. Ceely what's-her-name's party. The one Quint wants us to go to," she added when there was no recognition in Ginny's face. "Remember?"

No, she hadn't remembered. She'd dismissed it as soon as it had been mentioned, thinking it was just so much rhetoric. Just Quint giving lip service to helping "reform" her sister.

Obviously not.

But then, she'd learned that Quint didn't give lip service to anything. He didn't say what he didn't mean. There weren't many men like that. None that she knew, at any rate.

She folded her own clothes on top of Jenny's. Zoe had given them some clothing that Morgan had left behind. Quint's sister looked to be close to the same size as they were, which was lucky, since she didn't fancy wearing the same thing day in, day out, and shopping locally didn't exactly hold a lure for her.

Glancing now at her sister, she said, "I think he meant you."

"No, he meant us." Wearing an old T-shirt Kent had donated to the cause, Jenny slid her legs under the covers. "And him." She looked at Ginny, a grin playing on her lips. "Know what I think?"

Ginny felt tired tonight, bone tired. She'd put in a long day, putting Jake and Zoe's affairs in order. Stretching, she murmured, "No, what?"

"I think he likes you. A lot."

The comment froze her for a second before she turned to fix Jenny with a dismissive glance. "You're letting your imagination run away with you."

"No, I'm not." Jenny wasn't accustomed to noticing things about other people, but the more she thought about it, the more it made sense. "He looks at you like…like Jake looks at Zoe."

Ginny stopped brushing her hair and tossed aside the brush. "He does not look at me in any manner close to the way Jake looks at Zoe."

"Does, too." She knew what she saw. And there was more. "And you look at him when he's not watching. But I am."

Maybe she had looked at him a time or two, but that didn't prove anything. "For somebody who's being kept very busy, you seem to have an awful lot of time on your hands for staring."

A defensive tone would have normally been enough to put Jenny at odds with her sister. She'd squared off with far less provocation.

This time, she merely shrugged. "Just at the table." Her eyes danced as she watched her sister squirm. Jenny congratulated herself for hitting the nail on the head. "Know what else I think?"

Ginny braced herself. "No, what?"

Jenny lay down, snuggling under the covers. "We could do worse than stay in a place like this."

That was *not* what she'd expected Jenny to say. Not even close.

"A place like this?" Ginny echoed. Maybe she was hearing things. "You couldn't wait to leave Smoke Tree. You didn't even want to look back, remember?"

She refused to be encumbered by the past, for whatever reason. "I was nine. Besides, Serendipity's nothing like Smoke Tree was."

Ginny couldn't believe she was hearing this. Had her sister gone through a complete transformation, or was this because of some crush she'd developed on this Billy person?

"What about your friends?" Ginny pressed. "The people you said you couldn't live without."

There'd been more than one fight over that, over the kind of people she hung out with. Now she seemed willing just to walk away from them. Ginny didn't know whether to laugh or cry.

Her eyes shut, Jenny moved one restless shoulder in acknowledgment of the question. She debated answering her sister then decided that Ginny *had* gone through a lot for her. She and Carly had had a long talk about that, about the sacrifices family members had made for them. It had opened her eyes a little, talking to someone closer to her own age about it. Maybe Ginny was entitled to this.

"They didn't seem too torn up about me leaving." Very slowly, almost in slow motion, she turned to look at her sister. "Ginny?"

Ginny settled in beside her. The tone Jenny took had her slightly leery. Was something wrong? "Yes?"

"I'm…" She took a deep breath and tried again. "I'm sorry."

That Ginny's mouth didn't drop open was only because she willed it not to. "For what?"

Jenny didn't want to be pressed. "Just that. I'm sorry, okay? It's no big deal." She looked at Ginny. "Oh, damn, you're not going to cry, are you?"

Ginny sniffed, reaching for the tissue box on the nightstand. "Maybe I am."

"I shouldn't have said anything." Disgruntled, Jenny burrowed herself into the bed.

But Ginny wasn't willing to let it drop, not yet. "Don't you understand, this is the first time you *have* said something to me in a very long while. I'm crying because I'm happy."

Jenny dismissed the explanation with a snort, but it was obvious even to the casual eye that it pleased her that she meant so much to her sister. That made her sorrier than ever for her previous behavior. "Never understood that."

Ginny laughed softly, wanting to hug Jenny, knowing that it was too soon. "Give yourself a couple of years. It'll come to you."

Turning on her side, Jenny shut her eyes. "Boy, I hope not."

She pretended to already be asleep as she felt Ginny lightly stroke her head.

The last time she'd seen Jenny fussing like this, she'd been getting ready to go heaven only knew where and with whom. She certainly hadn't managed to get it out of her, even under the threat of being grounded.

This time it was for a party she knew that Jenny would have turned her nose up and jeered at only a short while ago. Now she actually sounded as if she was looking forward to it, although Jenny did sneak a glance her way every so often and tried to tone down her words.

The nonchalant pose wasn't taking. Jenny gave it up. She turned around for Ginny's benefit. "So, how do I look?"

She was wearing her jeans and a fresh shirt, as well as a smile. "Like someone who's about to have a good time tonight."

Jenny lit up like a candle, looking for all the world like the sister she had lost touch with a few years ago. And she had Quint to thank. Quint and his parents and the general-store owner and Carly...the list, Ginny realized, was a long one.

She accompanied Jenny down the stairs, if *accompanied* could be the right word. The girl went bounding down, practically taking two steps at a time.

Definitely happy, Ginny thought.

It seemed ironic to her that they had to escape one small town to find their future and return to another to find their souls.

Quint was at the bottom of the stairs, waiting for them. Was it her imagination, or was he looking even better now than earlier? She found herself looking forward to seeing him more and more the less time they had left in Serendipity. In just a few days, Jenny's so-called "sentence" would be up. After that, they probably would never see the Cutlers again.

Or Quint.

Why did her heart tighten like that? It shouldn't. And yet, it did.

"All set to go?" Quint's smile of approval washed over Jenny, but it was Ginny he was asking.

He was waiting for her to answer, she realized. "Me? No, I've decided not to go." She'd only feel out of place with all those people, anyway.

To her surprise, Quint caught her by the hand and drew her away from the foot of the stairs. "Sorry, you have no say in the matter. I intend to take both the Marlow sisters to this party."

Ginny looked over her shoulder at Zoe. "Has he always been this bossy?"

Zoe nodded solemnly as Jake came up to join her. "'Fraid so. Making him sheriff just made him more so."

"I have nothing to wear," she protested.

Quint wouldn't budge. Instead, his eyes languidly moved over her. She more than did justice to Morgan's jeans. "What you have on is fine. Clothes are clothes."

Typical male response. What wasn't typical was the way she felt in response to his gaze. Ginny was torn. She had to admit that part of her wanted to go, wanted to experience as much as she could with Quint before it was all over for good.

"I guess to avoid bloodshed I should go?"

Quint had known all along that he was going to win this argument. "Guess so." He ushered her out before she could say another word on the subject.

Zoe turned to Jake, a satisfied smile on her face. "What do you think?"

Jake knew that look. Knew, too, what he'd been watching happen in his own house. "I think someone's finally lit a fire under that boy." He laughed, turning away from the door. "I always wanted a lawyer in the family. Looks like I just might get my wish."

His chuckle vibrated along his wife's neck as he encircled her waist from behind and nuzzled her.

"You know, Zoe, we've got the house to ourselves for a few hours. Does that give you any ideas?"

She curled into his arms. "Lots of them."

They went up the stairs together, reaching the landing before Quint had pulled his car out of the driveway.

10

Amid the laughter that surrounded the evening, there was a kernel of sadness that sat at the heart of it, refusing to disappear, refusing to be ignored no matter how hard she tried.

Ginny had never been in the throes of both emotions before, happy and sad at the same time. She felt like a ball at a tennis match, stuck in perpetual motion, eternally being lobbed over the net, first to one side, then to the other.

The people gathered at Ceely Watts's birthday party were nothing like the people she'd known when she was growing up. Nothing like the people she'd expected. They'd greeted her and her sister not like strangers, but like new friends to be acquired.

For once, the easy atmosphere succeeded in stripping away her guard a layer at a time. And did it rather quickly.

It was an evening she'd always remember. She listened to stories being swapped, danced with Quint, sang "Happy Birthday" at the top of her lungs, eaten cake and then clambered up to the top of a huge hay mound, sinking into it as easily as she sank into Quint's arms. It helped that he was there beside her.

Helped and hindered.

She might have climbed onto a haystack, but she was on the emotional roller coaster of her life.

Under ordinary circumstances, between the slow pace the horse took, the moonlight and the quiet murmur of other couples, she would have fallen asleep. But not with Quint's arms wrapped comfortably around her. That burrowed excitement in the midst of easy contentment.

"Guess what?"

Her skin tingled as his breath drifted along her flesh. She felt goose bumps form instantly. Felt, too, the smile that was on his lips as it curved beside her cheek. "Hmm?"

"I think you have finally gotten the knack of relaxing," he whispered against her ear. *Or at least made some headway toward it,* he added silently.

If he only knew, she thought. Everything within her was poised like a tuning fork that had just been struck on the side of a half-filled glass of water the instant his breath touched her.

"It's hard to stay rigid on a pile of hay." She'd been resting her head against his shoulder, absorbing every sensation, every breath like an industrious squirrel saving nuts for the winter. The winter that stretched endlessly before her. The one when she was going to have to do without him. "I'm really going to be sorry to see this all end."

His arm tightened about her waist. He looked at the three other couples on the wagon. The quarters were close, but each behaved as if they were oblivious to the others. That included Ginny's sister and Billy Travis. Nice kid, Billy.

"I could get Simon to drive us around for another hour," he offered.

How about forever? The question was foolish and she bit it back.

"I don't mean the hayride, I mean all of it. Being here. I haven't had a vacation since—" Ginny paused, thinking. "I've never had a vacation," she realized out loud. No matter what had brought it about, the time she'd spent here had been wonderful.

He brought his cheek to rest beside hers. "This doesn't have to be a vacation, you know."

Could he feel it? Could he feel how he made her heart speed up, then skip a beat? Did he realize what he was doing to her? "What do you mean?"

Quint had already broached the subject once, earlier in the week. He was more serious than ever this time. "This could be forever, a way of life."

He was talking crazy, Ginny thought. "Right, give up working at the law firm, give up a possible junior partnership and move out here." She'd worked too long and too hard to walk away from that. Hadn't she?

"Why not?"

For a moment, as her mind came up against the simple question, she was speechless. And then she realized that he had to be joking. "And do what?" She laughed. "Go for hayrides the rest of my life? I'll forget how to walk."

She didn't think he was serious, he realized. "Why not be a lawyer—in between hayrides?"

"A lawyer—" She twisted in his arms to look at him. "You mean here?"

"I mean here. We don't have a lawyer in Serendipity," he reminded her. "With the town growing, I think it's high time we had one. A pretty one."

Now she knew he wasn't serious. For a moment, just a tiny, wild moment, she'd almost entertained the idea. "Is that a requirement?"

He pressed a kiss to her forehead, setting her heart fluttering like a freshly minted butterfly leaving its cocoon. "For me."

She would have laughed if she had the breath for it—but he'd managed to snatch that away. "I'd think you'd be surrounded by enough pretty girls already."

"None that I noticed."

So, he was capable of lying, too, was he? Just when she'd thought she'd found the one honest man left on God's earth. Showed what she knew.

"Yeah, right."

Fingertip beneath her chin, he turned her head

toward him. "None," he emphasized again, "that I noticed. Until now."

If her heart was hammering any harder, it was going to fall right out into the hay. "You expect me to believe that?"

His eyes held hers. "I expect," he said softly, "you to believe me. A woman should believe the man who's about to ask her to marry him—otherwise, how is she to take the proposal seriously?"

There was a wild buzzing going on in her ears. Ginny stiffened. He was mocking her, she realized. Making fun at her expense. He had to be. Proposals didn't just drop out of the sky like this. Just when she'd finally begun to trust him.

"She isn't," Ginny retorted.

Without knowing where she was, only that she wanted, *needed,* to get away, Ginny surprised Quint by suddenly sliding off the slow-moving haystack on the wagon bed and tumbling to the ground.

"Ginny, stop."

But she scrambled to her feet, ignoring his cries as she began to run. Into the darkness. Away from him.

"Stop the damn wagon," Quint ordered.

Stunned, six pairs of eyes turned to look at Quint. He pressed his lips together to keep back the ripe oath on his tongue.

"Wait here," Quint instructed the driver.

"Go after her, Quint," Jenny begged. Squinting,

she was having a hard time making Ginny out as she ran up the road.

"I fully intend to, Jenny. I fully intend to." It was a promise he meant to keep.

Jumping off the wagon, Quint broke into a run, afraid of losing sight of her.

"Ginny, stop. For God's sake, stop running," he yelled after her disappearing form.

Instead, he saw her speed up. Quint swallowed another curse. Shouting it wouldn't help anything. Damn fool woman, what had gotten into her? What had he said to scare her away like that?

She was fast, he realized. Faster than he would have thought. But he was faster, and he caught up to her in a matter of a few minutes. He expected her to slow down, but she didn't. Instead, she poured on one last burst of speed.

"Go away!" she cried over her shoulder.

"Can't."

Running abreast of her, Quint made a grab for her arm when she refused to stop. He caught her forearm. Ginny tried to pull away and they both tumbled to the ground, their bodies tangling as they went down.

Quint was quick to take advantage of the situation and got on top of her. He straddled her, his legs around both sides of her body so she couldn't get away. Ginny squirmed beneath him, trying to throw him off. She tensed when she saw the slow, lazy smile that spread along his mouth.

"I don't suggest you do that." Leaning over, he caught her wrists to keep her from taking a swing at him. "Otherwise we'll be facing a whole other problem if you keep wiggling."

"Get off me," she ordered.

He didn't budge. "Only if you promise not to run off like that."

She looked as if she was debating, weighing her chances of flight. His hands tightened on her wrists, pressing them against the ground. She was trapped.

Grudgingly, she nodded. "I promise."

Quint was on his feet in a minute. Not about to take any chances, he kept one of her wrists prisoner. He didn't feel like engaging in another footrace just yet. She might win this time.

"You know—" he pulled her to her feet "—for a lawyer you don't act very logically."

Ginny tried to yank her wrist free and got nowhere. "Why, because I should have fallen to my knees because you proposed?"

Did she really think he expected her to react like that? "No, because you went running off into the night like that." He knew she didn't know her way around. "Do you have any idea where you are?"

"No." It cost her to admit it, even though they both knew that she didn't have a clue where she was.

It took effort to contain his anger and not shake her. He could have lost her. Permanently. "Do you have any idea how lost you could have gotten in a matter of minutes?''

She turned away, brushing off her clothes. Her shoulder ached from where it had made contact with the ground. ''I don't need a lecture.''

His words enveloped her. ''What you need is a man to love you.''

''Jumping into bed, right,'' she bit off. ''That'll solve everything.''

He turned her around to face him. ''A man to love you,'' Quint repeated, emphasizing the word *love,* ''not *make* love to you. There's a difference. One leads to the other, but the order's the important thing here. Don't get it confused.''

She raised her chin, tossing her head. ''And you're volunteering for the job?''

He nodded once slowly. ''Hand raised high in the air.''

She refused to believe him. How could she? ''To love me.'' She said each word deliberately as if they were somehow obscure.

There was no hesitation. ''Yes.''

She didn't know what he was up to, but she wasn't buying it. Pushing past him, she began walking away again. ''Don't do me any favors.''

''I figured it would be mutual.'' This time the words, rather than Quint, stopped her. Turning, she looked at him sharply. ''The favors, I mean.'' Coming closer, he studied her face, looking for a clue. ''What are you afraid of, Geneva?''

She squared her shoulders, on the defensive. "I'm not afraid."

"Yes, you are." She wasn't going to talk or brazen her way out of this, lawyer or no lawyer. He wanted the truth. "You bolted off that hayride like a deer with the first smell of man in its nostrils at the height of hunting season."

"I just wanted to get away from a crazy person. Fear had nothing to do with it." She saw he wasn't buying her explanation. "You're imagining things."

"Am I?" He was willing to hear her out if she'd tell him the truth. "Then why did you jump off the wagon and run blindly off like that? That spells fear in my book."

Ginny didn't give a damn about his book, she wanted what was left of her pride back. "Look, I don't know why you just asked me—"

Maybe it was a joke or a bet he'd made with someone. Or maybe he just felt sorry for her, she didn't know, but none of that was enough of a reason for him to have done what he'd done. Hinting that he was going to propose to her was just plain cruel.

"Don't you?" He was as calm as she was agitated, and that only made her more so. "I would have thought the reason was obvious." Quint placed his hands on her shoulders to hold her in place. "I'm in love with you, Ginny."

She could only stare at him. "You can't be."

Why wouldn't she believe him? "I know my own mind. I know that something happened the very first time I saw you storm into my office, breathing fire, tossing that wild hair of yours around, making me want to run my fingers through it. Making me wonder what a woman like you would feel like if I held her in my arms." His eyes soften as he looked at her. "And when I found out, then I knew."

Ginny felt nerves pulling taut within her. "Knew what?"

"That I wanted you in my arms forever." Very slowly he ran his hands along her arms, emotions charging through him that were almost too intense to corral. "Now, why did you run?"

She pressed her lips together, telling herself she wasn't going to cry because then he'd really think she was crazy. He probably did already. What sane person jumped from a moving wagon? But there was a reason for that. And he'd been right about that, too.

"All right," she admitted finally, "I am afraid."

He tried to read the look in her eyes and didn't quite succeed. "Of me?"

"In a way," she allowed slowly. The words came out in measured clusters. "Of how it would feel if I said yes and then it turned out to be a big joke."

What Quint felt was so strong, he'd just taken for granted that she would know. He realized that he'd been wrong. He had to move slowly. But it was hard when everything inside him wanted to rush. He wanted to embrace what was happening, to let everyone in on it. He hadn't thought that he'd have to start with her.

"It's not—"

But she placed the tips of her fingers to his mouth. She wasn't finished. "Or worse, that it's not a big joke, that you're serious."

He took her hand from his lips and held it in both of his. The expression on his face was earnest. "I think you just lost me."

She tried very hard to explain, to let him into the jumble in her mind. It wasn't easy explaining fear, or letting him see this part of her.

"That you're serious for now. For tonight, maybe even for a day, a month, a whole year. And then you'll change your mind." She closed her eyes, pressing back the tears that suddenly wanted to come. "You'll leave because you can't stay. Because you want to be somewhere else, with someone else, someplace other than with me," she whispered.

Moved, Quint gently took her face in his hands and looked into her eyes. He understood now, understood that he was confronting the whole woman, and part of that confrontation involved the little girl who'd been abandoned by her father, who had periodically been deposited in a string of foster homes whenever her mother got the wanderlust, or tired of her and used the excuse that she couldn't properly care for her any longer. The little girl who'd endured one strange home after another, passed from one to the other like so much unwanted laundry. The girl who'd been determined that her sister wouldn't have to put up with the emptiness that came of knowing you were being abandoned.

All those things had gone into forming her, into making her the woman that he now loved. The woman who was afraid to believe in that love.

He did his best to set her at ease, to make her trust him.

"I'm not like your mother, or your father, or anyone else who's been in your life before, Ginny." He looked into her eyes and spoke to her soul. "I love you. It's a fact of life. A fact of *my* life. Hopefully, a fact of your life.

"And I'm not going to change my mind. Not in an hour, or a day, or a week, or the thousand weeks that'll follow that. Ask anyone. I make up my mind and it stays made up."

She wanted, oh so much, to believe him. "And your heart? Does it stay made up, too?"

Taking her hand in his, he placed it over his chest. She could feel it beating hard. Excitement built within her.

"It stays made up, too. And it's made up now. I can't make you stay, Ginny, not if you want to go. Not if you don't feel the same about me as I do you. But that doesn't change the way I feel about you. If you walk away, I'll still go on loving you."

"But why, why do you love me?" She needed reasons, to know.

Love couldn't be explained, not really. Quint knew that, but he did his best because she needed to hear reasons.

"Because I just do. Because you're kind. Because you could have walked away from your sister so many times and you didn't. Because you have love in your heart. Because you're a fighter and you survived even when the odds were against you. Because of the spark that came into your eyes when you took on my parents' fight and made it your own.

"And because—" his voice softened "—when I hold you, when I kiss you, there's nothing left of this earth but you and me. Nobody's ever made the world disappear for me before, Ginny. And nobody ever will again."

He was making her a promise. And she believed him. "Nobody's ever said anything like this to me before."

"Good." He brushed the hair away from her face, wanting just to look at her. "I like being the first. So, what do you say?"

She bit her lip. "I'm still afraid." But her eyes were the eyes of a woman who was conquering her fears.

"I'll be there with you, every step of the way," he promised her. Taking her into his arms, he held her to him, his words feathering through her hair. "Through the vows, the kids, the grandkids—"

Maybe she was getting hysterical, she thought. If

she was, it felt good. Laughter bubbled up inside her. "Wait, wait for me to catch up."

"I'll wait, Ginny." He grew serious. "The rest of my life if I have to."

"You won't have to." She threaded her arms around his neck, leaning into his body. This was where she was meant to be. Drawing her courage to her, she told him what she knew was in her heart, what she'd been afraid to let free. "I love you, Quint." She let out a sigh, then looked at him. "That's just about the bravest thing I've ever said."

He understood. It was brave because she'd put her heart at risk. "Nothing sexier than a brave woman, I always say." His mouth curved into a confident smile. It was going to be all right. "Marry me?"

"Try and stop me."

"Wouldn't dream of it." He had other dreams, he thought as his mouth found hers. And those were just about to begin.

* * * * *

Watch for Morgan's story,
A MATCH FOR MORGAN,
coming to Silhouette Yours Truly
in March 1999.

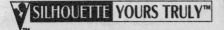
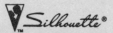

FORTUNE'S *Children*™

**The Fortune family requests
the honor of your presence at the weddings of**

FORTUNE'S CHILDREN™

The Brides

Silhouette Desire's scintillating new miniseries,
featuring the beloved Fortune family
and five of your favorite authors.

***The Honor Bound Groom*—January 1999**
by Jennifer Greene (SD #1190)

***Society Bride*—February 1999**
by Elizabeth Bevarly (SD #1196)

And look for more **FORTUNE'S CHILDREN:
THE BRIDES** installments by Leanne Banks,
Susan Crosby and Merline Lovelace,
coming in spring 1999.

Available at your favorite retail outlet.

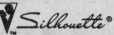

Silhouette®

Follow That Baby

FOLLOW THAT BABY...

the fabulous cross-line series featuring the infamously wealthy Wentworth family...continues with:

THE MERCENARY AND THE NEW MOM

by Merline Lovelace
(Intimate Moments, 2/99)

No sooner does Sabrina Jensen's water break than she's finally found by the presumed-dead father of her baby: Jack Wentworth. But their family reunion is put on hold when Jack's past catches up with them....

Available at your favorite retail outlet, only from

Silhouette®

THE MacGREGORS ARE BACK!

#1 *New York Times* bestselling author

NORA ROBERTS

Presents...

THE MacGREGORS:
Alan—Grant
February 1999

Will Senator Alan MacGregor be
able to help Shelby Campbell conquer
her fear of his high-profile life-style?
And will Grant Campbell and
Gennie Grandeau find that their love
is too strong to keep them apart?
Find out by reading the exciting
and touching *The MacGregors:
Alan—Grant* by Nora Roberts.

Coming soon in
Silhouette Special Edition:
**March 1999: THE PERFECT
NEIGHBOR (SE#1232)**

Also, watch for the MacGregor stories where it all began
in the next exciting 2-in-1 volume!
April 1999: THE MacGREGORS: Daniel—Ian

Available at your favorite retail outlet, only from

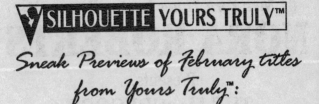

SILHOUETTE YOURS TRULY™

Sneak Previews of February titles from Yours Truly™:

WEDDING? IMPOSSIBLE!
Weddings, Inc.
by Karen Templeton

Zoe needed one thing to make her life perfectly peaceful—to get her matchmaking mother to stop pushing her down the aisle! So in exasperation, Zoe agreed to the blind date her family had set up. She figured this might be the perfect thing to get her mind off her gorgeous, available—but antimarriage—business nemesis, Mike. She was all set to meet her mystery man—until she started to find out more about him. Like he was gorgeous, available…and had a business nemesis named Zoe.…

BACHELORETTE BLUES
by Robyn Amos

The chain letter promising true love was a joke…right? Shayna Gunther already had her true love picked out—in fact, she had three of them on her list of potential Mr. Rights. Just because her well-ordered life had turned upside down when she threw the letter away didn't mean a thing. But when sexy Max Winston showed up, maybe it was time for Shayna to rethink her Mr. Right list—and start searching her apartment for that letter!